"Dear girl," I murmured, once we were clear of Acharro's *residencia* and in the charge of Suncha, "you took a terrible risk, stirring him up like that. For all his Cambridge education, he might have handed us our heads."

"I doubt it," said Vesper. "I don't think head-hunting is a Chirican custom. Our heads are perfectly safe. All the more since Acharro thinks there's something useful in mine. I wish there were."

"Good heavens," I cried, "and you told Acharro you had a plan!"

"No," said Vesper. "I only asked him what he'd say if I did."

LLOYD ALEXANDER, a resident of Drexel Hill, Pennsylvania, is the author of *Westmark, The Kestrel, The Beggar Queen,* The Prydain Chronicles, including *The Book of Three, The Black Cauldron* (a Newbery Honor Book), *The Castle of Llyr, Taran Wanderer,* and *The High King* (winner of the Newbery Medal), and *The Illyrian Adventure,* to which this book is a sequel. He has also written *The Foundling and Other Tales of Prydain, The First Two Lives of Lukas-Kasha, Time Cat, The Wizard in the Tree,* and *The Town Cats and Other Tales.* All are available in Dell Yearling editions.

The El Dorado Adventure

LLOYD ALEXANDER

LAUREL-LEAF BOOKS bring together under a single imprint outstanding works of fiction and nonfiction particularly suitable for young adult readers, both in and out of the classroom. Charles F. Reasoner, Professor Emeritus of Children's Literature and Reading, New York University, is consultant to this series.

Published by
Dell Publishing Co., Inc.
1 Dag Hammarskjold Plaza
New York, New York 10017

ISBN: 0-440-20068-7

RL: 7.4

Reprinted by arrangement with E. P. Dutton, a division of NAL, Penguin, Inc.

Printed in the United States of America

March 1988

10 9 8 7 6 5 4 3 2 1

KRI

for other Vespers

The El Dorado Adventure

Map by Meryl Rosner

CHAPTER 1

Miss Vesper Holly is the only Philadelphian of my acquaintance to own a volcano. I can think of no one better suited to deal with explosive real estate. Despite her accomplishments in languages, art, music, science, and mathematics, the dear girl finds eruptions and other nerve-shattering events irresistibly magnetic.

"It's not much of a volcano. Hardly Mount Vesuvius." Vesper looked disappointed. "Besides, Brinnie, it's dead as a doornail."

I was relieved to hear that.

"It's called Ocotalpa," said Vesper. "That's a Chirican Indian name, isn't it? Anyhow, it's extinct. Look, it says so right here."

She handed me a surveyor's map and went back to rummaging through the papers scattered over the library table and floor. Her vigorous, orderly intelligence is not always revealed by her behavior.

"Found it," Vesper called out. "Here's the deed, the

land title, receipts, *derechos de propiedad.* All in all, including the volcano—there's a lake, too—it's a fair-sized chunk in the middle of El Dorado. *El Dorado,* 'the realm of gold'! What do you say to that, Brinnie?"

"I can tell you one thing," I answered. "The name means a wild goose chase. The old conquistadores thought they had discovered a realm of gold—El Dorado. It turned out they were wrong."

I went on to explain that the present Republic of El Dorado, freed from Spanish domination by *El Libertador,* the patriot Simón Bolívar, was one of a tumble of countries crowding the neck of land between North and South America. Far from being a realm of gold, its natural resources consisted mainly of a climate hotter than Philadelphia pepperpot, sweltering jungles, aggressive insects, and disagreeable tropical ailments.

True, not every day does a girl barely turned seventeen suddenly find herself possessor of extensive holdings in the wilds of Central America. Even so, I could not generate much heartfelt enthusiasm.

Vesper, of course, was gleeful. Her green eyes brightened with keener interest than she had shown in anything all winter. "The property starts upriver from Puerto Palmas"—she traced a finger over the map—"where the Rio Culebra makes a sort of big, loopy oxbow. I never knew Father owned anything like it."

Nor did I, though I should have. Let me briefly explain.

My dear wife, Mary, and I, Professor Brinton Garrett, had been named Vesper's guardians by my old friend and traveling companion, the late Dr. Benjamin Rittenhouse Holly. By her own special mixture of cajolery, browbeating, and willpower, Vesper had installed us as permanent guests in the mansion of her Strafford estate near Philadelphia. My responsibilities included her proper upbringing and the organization of Holly's papers.

Neither task had been completed.

As for Vesper's upbringing, she continued to manage that herself without any guidance whatever.

As for the papers, Holly had been an intrepid explorer, a brilliant archeologist, a daring adventurer—and a disaster at keeping his personal business in order. Unconcerned with humdrum details, he left a hodgepodge of notes, letters, and diaries that defied description, let alone organization.

Not surprisingly, I was unaware of such holdings. Vesper had interrupted my labors the year before, when our excursion to the kingdom of Illyria nearly cost us our lives. I had, since then, made little headway through the swamp of documents. I offer this not as an excuse but merely a clarification.

"Father piled up more fortunes by accident than anybody ever did on purpose," Vesper went on. "When you two were in the Punjab, slogging across a riverbed, didn't he stub his toe on a diamond big as a goose egg?"

"Yes," I replied, "and gave it away to a passing Untouchable. Your father said the fellow looked as if he needed a pleasant surprise."

"I call that real style," said Vesper. "According to the documents, he won all this land in a poker game."

"That happened long before we met," I said. "It would be typical of him. Your father was always lucky. He was never cautious."

"He counted on you for caution," Vesper said. "He couldn't have done without his dear old Brinnie."

"I certainly would have kept him from games of chance," I said. "In this case, his luck brought him nothing. Look at the survey. The area isn't suitable for coffee bushes, rubber trees, or banana plantations. Dear girl, the property is worthless."

"Then what about the telegram?" Vesper retrieved this communication from Moggie, her large orange cat, who had been sleeping on it. She paced the floor, reading the phrases aloud. "Urgent . . . sail to Puerto Palmas . . . El Dorado estate . . . immediate attention. Passage on *City of Brotherly Love* paid in advance."

A certain eagerness in her tone made me suspect what she had in mind. She could not, I protested, even consider dashing off to some fever-ridden backwater because of a few cryptic words from an anonymous individual.

"Not anonymous," replied Vesper. "The telegram's signed Alain de Rochefort. He sounds French."

"Worse yet," I said.

Vesper perched on a corner of the table and dangled her long legs. "Well, Brinnie, what shall we do?"

"What *we* shall do is nothing." I carefully explained that the only reasonable and businesslike procedure was to put the whole matter in the hands of her lawyers. They could dispatch one of their people as Vesper's representative or get in touch with a reliable local agent.

"And miss an ocean cruise? Even if it comes to nothing, it's fascinating. A rendezvous with a mysterious Frenchman —" Vesper stopped and gave me a frown of concern. "You know, Brinnie, you've been looking pale and peaky these days. A little sunlight and salt air would do you a world of good."

More beneficial, I replied, would be my continuing work on her father's papers, not to mention my neglected history of the Etruscans. Vesper had begun experiments in fractionating hydrocarbons. Instead of contemplating meetings with unknown and probably untrustworthy foreigners, she could better spend her time in the laboratory.

At Vesper's urging, however, I did drive to Philadelphia later that morning and made inquiries at the shipping office. Though I gained no information about de Rochefort himself, it was a fact that prepaid, first-class passage had been booked for us on the sidewheel steamer.

I also visited the law firm of Kenge & Carboy. The senior attorneys were absent, but I left word instructing them to look into all details of the El Dorado situation at their very earliest convenience.

It was evening by the time I returned to Strafford. Mary was waiting for me. She looked concerned.

"Brinnie," she began, taking my hand, "do you feel quite well? I've noticed you've been looking a touch pale and peaky. A little salt air and sunlight would really do you a world of good. Vesper, too. The dear child needs some recreation."

I was about to disagree when Vesper appeared with Moggie draped over her shoulder.

"I thought I heard you come in. Aunt Mary and I had a lovely talk this afternoon."

"I gather." I took the opportunity then to report my day's activities. I assured Vesper that all had been set in motion in the most practical way, and advised her to put further speculation from her thoughts. Even assuming we had wished to accept this most unlikely invitation, the *City of Brotherly Love* was due to depart within a scant two days.

"Too bad." Vesper shrugged. "You're a genius at organizing things, but that's not enough time to get ready, even for you."

At this, perhaps I bridled a little. As Vesper well knew, I did have some long experience. Preparations would be hasty, not as thorough as I preferred, but not beyond the realm of possibility.

"Oh?" said Vesper. "Good. Settled. We'll be in Puerto Palmas—"

"My dear girl," I broke in, "I was speaking only theoretically."

"My dear old Brinnie." Vesper smiled. There was a slight but unmistakable resemblance between her expression and that of Moggie. "I'd be lost without you."

We embarked with time to spare. Once out of the port of Philadelphia, we could do little but enjoy the niceties of this most modern vessel.

Mornings, we lingered over sumptuous breakfasts, then strolled the polished deck, chatting with the officers and the few passengers, most of whom were bound for Venezuela and Brazil. Afternoons, we reclined on deck chairs and waited for the white-clad steward to bring our tea tray. Braiding up her marmalade-colored hair, Vesper had taken possession of one of my cloth caps and cocked it over her eyes to shade them against the high southern sun.

"Whoever may be our mysterious Frenchman," she remarked, "he set us up well."

Indeed, our staterooms were luxurious, our food excellent and abundant, the service impeccable. My original objections evaporated under cloudless skies and refreshing breezes. The pleasantly uneventful voyage, the rolling of the sea, lulled us into a comfortable, almost indolent mood. Vesper, this time, had been correct, I freely admitted. A cruise in southern waters offered the best cure for a Philadelphia February.

Vesper, whose curiosity would normally have driven her to activity, appeared content to bask lazily. But her mind was not idle.

"I'm looking forward to meeting our benefactor," she remarked after we sighted the Golfo Dorado and the captain announced an early landing in Puerto Palmas. "I'll have a question or two for him."

Our business, I was confident, could be of no great importance. I assured her we would conclude it without difficulty.

"I don't mean that," replied Vesper. "I was thinking about the passage fare."

I reminded her it had been paid, and we certainly could find no fault with our accommodations.

"It never struck you, Brinnie? One-way tickets!"

Vesper yawned and settled in her chair for an untroubled nap.

I could not do likewise.

CHAPTER 2

"The only thing missing is de Rochefort." Vesper poked her nose into the basket of orchids and inhaled loudly. "They're beautiful. Even so, I'd rather see him than his flowers."

We were not to be given that opportunity, not, at least, in the immediate future. Before embarking, Vesper had sent a telegram asking him to meet us at the pier. There had been no sign of the fellow.

Instead, as we stepped off the gangway, Vesper was recognized and ceremoniously welcomed by a *mandadero* from—as he claimed—the most luxurious hotel in Puerto Palmas. Thanks to our absent host, customs formalities had been waived. We squeezed our baggage and ourselves into a small cart drawn by an even smaller burro. We were accompanied along the way by a parade of an especially long-legged variety of local chickens. Though nothing in the capital was far from anything else, our leisurely pace made our journey seem longer.

"We'd have gone faster with the chickens pulling us," remarked Vesper when at last we reached our destination: a tile-roofed, Spanish-style building on the spacious but unpaved central square, Plaza Bolívar. Like our steamer passage, our lodgings had been arranged and paid in advance. Escorting us up to our apartments, the proprietor transmitted the deepest regrets of Señor de Rochefort. The *caballero* had been called away unexpectedly. We were begged to make ourselves comfortable.

"That should be easy to do." Vesper glanced happily around the rooms. They were, in fact, better than I would have supposed, with whitewashed plaster walls, slatted blinds, a balcony allowing a view of the surrounding sweep of palm trees that had given the capital its name.

In addition to the flowers on the table, a basket of bananas, mangoes, and melons awaited us. Vesper scanned the accompanying card.

" 'Compliments and apologies from A. de R.' " Vesper immediately attacked one of the mangoes. "Does he figure on keeping us busy eating until he turns up?"

If so, I observed, he might arrive momentarily. Vesper's appetite has always functioned at a high degree of efficiency. In any case, we could only follow the suggestion of our host and wait patiently.

"I'll be patient later," said Vesper, wiping her chin on her sleeve. "First, we need some lighter clothes."

Though I had packed our summer garments, I agreed that even those would be constrictive in the El Dorado climate. Accordingly, we ventured out and across the deserted plaza. As a center of fashionable elegance, Puerto Palmas was not Philadelphia. Our Mr. Wanamaker's emporium had no counterpart along the duckboard walkways and arcades of canvas awnings.

Vesper did find one open shop, where I purchased a cork sun helmet and a pair of lightweight knickers. Vesper outfitted herself in a white linen jacket. She also scandalized the proprietor when she bought loose-fitting trousers and a wide-brimmed straw hat tied about the crown with a long red bandana.

By the time we emerged, the walkways had come alive with passersby. White-suited, puffing on thin cigars, colonials and Creoles of Spanish extraction strolled with their ladies sheltering under parasols. Soldiers from the local *cuartel* lounged on the corners.

Vesper's attention went more to the scattering of *indios* with glistening black hair and luminous dark eyes in bronze faces. The men dressed much alike in coarse cottons. The women of every age, however, displayed fringed skirts of vivid orange and green. Even the smallest girls carried pots, baskets, and all other burdens on their heads, moving with a remarkable grace and stately dignity.

"I want to learn how to do that." Vesper would have tried balancing a pot on her own head then and there had I not persuaded her otherwise. "Where did so many people come from all of a sudden?"

They had, I explained, been observing the custom of the afternoon siesta. We had been deprived of ours. I wished to correct that deficiency by returning to the hotel where, by now, we might have some further word from de Rochefort.

"If the business is as unimportant as you say, Brinnie, it can wait. If it's as important as he says, he'll find us one way or another. But," she added, "if you really can't do without your nap—"

Before that, Vesper insisted on our sampling a variety of delicacies from a street vendor. The dear girl has an esophagus of galvanized iron. Not similarly equipped, I should have known better.

"Brinnie, what's wrong? You've gone all red in the face."

Unable to voice a reply, I could only gesture that I would appreciate some large quantity of cold liquid.

"We'll get you something soothing," Vesper declared, while I gasped and mopped my brow. "An antidote for those chili peppers or whatever they were. They did have a little nip to them."

Our steps had taken us from the plaza and in the direction of the waterfront, a scatter of open sheds and palm-thatched warehouses. The heavy, humid combination of aromas assailed us: brackish water from the Culebra estuary, ripe bananas, damp vegetation, and antique fish. Vesper halted and cocked an ear. The sound of a guitar drifted from a cantina that resembled a large corncrib built onto a small barrelhouse.

"Just the place," said Vesper, attracted by the music. In my opinion, the presence of tourists, especially young females wearing trousers, would be frowned upon. Vesper had already pushed eagerly through the swinging doors.

The guitarist, a morose, unshaven fellow, sat on an upended crate atop what might be called a refreshment bar. Vesper was not frowned upon; her arrival drew only passing attention from the handful of what I judged to be merchant sailors off the couple of coasting vessels at the dock.

We seated ourselves at an empty table. Since no *mozo* came to take our order, Vesper offered to approach the bar herself. I considered it more seemly for me to do so. As we discussed this point of etiquette, we did not go unobserved.

An individual who had been eying us from the moment of our entry left his corner to ask if he could be of help. He was short, but thickset and muscular, with a sun-freckled bald dome rising from a fringe of grizzled hair. From his round, weathered face and faded denim shirt, I took him to be in the nautical profession.

"Smiler," he said cheerfully.

He was, I realized, identifying himself. He turned his pair of shrewd little blue eyes on Vesper, then on me.

"You, sir, and the young miss: Anglos?"

"Philadelphians," I corrected.

"Indeed you are! Indeed you are!" he exclaimed, as if he wished both to reassure us of that fact and congratulate us on it. He seized my hand, giving it a hearty shake, and did likewise to Vesper. In the process, he plumped himself down on the chair facing us.

"It's a pleasure to meet fellow citizens of our great Republic," he went on briskly. "It's my misfortune not to be a native of your city, but I am one of its most devoted admirers."

Vesper introduced us, then asked where he made his home. Mr. Smiler shrugged.

"Many places. My brother Slider and I haven't seen the States for twenty years, or thereabouts."

"You've never been back?" asked Vesper. "After all that time?"

"It would not be advisable." Our uninvited tablemate

sighed, then quickly reassumed his previous bright spirits. "Not advisable at all."

At this, I hoped Vesper would drop the matter. Naturally, she did not. She wished to know the reason for such inadvisability. "Trouble with the law?" she said hopefully.

"Only a judicial misunderstanding," said Smiler, "regarding some small items of property accidentally in our possession. Slider and I preferred not to argue the point."

"Now you both live in Puerto Palmas?"

"After a fashion. We live mostly on the Culebra. Or, to put it more exactly, on the *Libertador.* A riverboat, and a very trim little vessel she is."

"You're a pilot?"

"No, that's Slider's line of work, and the captain's. I'm chief engineer, among other things. It's a good life, the river trade—what there is of it."

Smiler leaned back in his chair. This talkative intruder had hinted at a past that was probably unlawful, or disreputable at best. Now he gave every sign of intending to favor us with more details. Worse yet, Vesper encouraged him. Much as I admire the dear child's lucid intellect and unflagging curiosity, I have always tried to dissuade her from striking up conversations with total strangers. Thus far, I have not succeeded.

"You must know the area pretty well," Vesper went on. "Did you ever hear of Ocotalpa?"

"The old volcano?" Smiler bobbed his head. "Heard of it, yes. It's inland a little. I've never seen it close up. We keep to the river. The Chiricas we trade with live mostly near the shore."

Vesper leaned forward and put her elbows on the table. "You mean there are still Chirican tribes?"

"Only one," said Smiler. "There used to be dozens. The Spanish conquistadores wiped out the others. In the old days, the *indios* worshipped that volcano. Slider's your man, though, if you want to know more about it."

Smiler cocked an eye at Vesper. "You've kindly inquired after our occupations, you won't mind if I ask the same of you. We don't see Anglos much, let alone Philadelphians. I wouldn't think you're on a pleasure trip."

"We aren't," said Vesper.

"Private business," I quickly put in, with some emphasis on the first word.

At the same time, I began to fear that the spicy food had affected my eyesight. Smiler suddenly appeared to be not only sitting in his chair but also standing beside himself.

"Why, here's Slider now," exclaimed Smiler, beaming at his exact duplicate, bald spot and all. The pair shook hands with greatest fraternal affection, as if they had not seen each other for years.

"You're twins." Vesper grinned with pleasure. "Wonderful!"

"So it is," replied Slider, in a voice exactly like that of his brother. "We're glad of it, Smiler and I. In foreign climes, surrounded by strangers, it's a comfort for us both."

"Miss Vesper was inquiring about the old Spanish days," said Smiler. "That's your line of country, Slider."

The twin drew a chair up to our table and installed himself as firmly as his brother. I murmured to Vesper that we should no longer delay our return. De Rochefort might be waiting for us even now. Though I had spoken barely above a whisper, the twins had equally sharp ears. Hearing the name, they raised their eyebrows to precisely the same degree and exchanged identical glances.

"You know de Rochefort?" Vesper was quite aware of the look that passed between the brothers.

"Who doesn't?" said Slider. "Smiler's the one who can tell you most about him."

"Indeed I can," said Smiler, "if, first, you don't mind my asking what might be your dealings with that fellow."

"We don't know yet," said Vesper. "We haven't met him."

"Ah." Smiler nodded. "Then I take it you haven't any notion—"

A bloodcurdling shriek burst from somewhere behind me, and a rasping voice bawled, "*¡Fuego! ¡Fuego! ¡Los diablos!* Shoot them!"

CHAPTER 3

Vesper had glanced up but did not move. Within the instant, as that ruffianly voice ordered open fire, I leaped from my chair and propelled myself toward her. The vigor of my protective gesture tumbled us both to the ground where I hauled her under the shelter of the table.

"Brinnie, for heaven's sake—"

The dear girl protested, but I kept a firm grip, shielding her with my person against the hail of bullets I expected from one moment to the next.

None came. The guitarist continued playing; the buzz of conversation was undiminished. I ventured to raise my head. The twin faces of Smiler and Slider observed me curiously from above.

Vesper, meanwhile, had disentangled herself and climbed to her feet. She peered under the table.

"What are you doing there, Brinnie?"

She extended her hand and helped me to crawl out. The patrons of the refreshment bar kept on about their business as if threats of shooting were everyday occurrences. My sun helmet had fallen to the floor. Still perplexed, I went to retrieve it, then drew back.

A scrawny green and yellow parrot perched on the rim. The creature turned a beady eye on me.

"¡A quema ropa! ¡Fuego!"

"That's Adelita," said Smiler.

"She's Captain O'Hara's," added Slider, "which means old Blazer himself won't be far behind."

Vesper made no comment about my unfortunate, though understandable, misjudgment. Adjusting my attire and composure, I stepped over to retrieve my headgear. The parrot now decided to occupy it as a nest. When I attempted to dislodge her, she opened a beak like a snapping turtle's and nipped at my fingers.

I hastily pulled back my hand. The impudent bird gave a cackling laugh, unseemly even for a parrot.

"Hello, sailor!" The garish fowl ruffled up the feathers around her neck. *"¡Mi corazón!"*

"I think she wants her head scratched," said Vesper. Seeing that I was unwilling to perform that service, Vesper bent down and put out a finger. Adelita clambered onto it with a certain raffish dignity, all the while jabbering a mixture of Spanish, English, and several incomprehensible Indian dialects.

"She's a Tower of Babel with feathers." Vesper fearlessly scratched around the powerful beak. "She only repeats what she hears, but she looks as if she really does know what she's saying."

The bird's bright orange eyes did seem to hold a wicked glint. Adelita's language was as gaudy as her plumage. I preferred not to speculate on where she had learned some of her comments.

"You've met the old harridan, have you now?"

The new arrival was a big, loose-limbed man with a grimy white yachting cap on the back of his head. His crust of beard had no doubt once been red but was now a pinkish gray. He was far from young, with a face so battered and sun-blackened I could not guess his age. He still looked to be a man of his hands, and I would not have wished to come within range of his fists. He had brawler written all over him.

"Blazer to his friends, bad news to his foes." He grinned at Vesper. "Blazer it is for you, *mavourneen.*"

Sighting him, Adelita flapped to his shoulder, ducking her head up and down. Vesper introduced us and—though I felt it unnecessary—explained what had happened.

Blazer barked out a laugh and clapped me on the shoulder. "Never mind, you're not the first she's frighted out of their wits. There was an old army sergeant loafing around here, and you should have seen the poor fellow duck for cover when she started her gab.

"She goes a bit mad sometimes," Blazer continued. "When the fit's on her, she'll play you the Battle of Puerto Palmas, bugle calls, the wounded screaming, the whole bloody business. *¡A quema ropa!* Point-blank! Fire! That's Bolívar himself giving the command when the Spaniards stormed our position. The old biddy was with me all through it. She's got it still stuck in her head."

"Poor Adelita," muttered the parrot. "*¡Hurrah! ¡Arriba!*"

"Simón Bolívar?" said Vesper. "You were with him?"

"That I was." Blazer straddled a chair. "A lad of eighteen, fresh out of County Mayo, with the troopers hot on my heels, wanting to hang me for a croppy rebel. I've not seen poor Ireland since." He chuckled. "There's a warrant still on me in Castlebar and everywhere else, I shouldn't wonder."

Vesper, I feared, had drawn us into undesirable company and the sooner out of it the better. Of course, she had to hear more. Blazer was all too willing to oblige.

"So, off I sailed and threw in with Bolívar," he went on. "Why not? Peons, *indios*—what are they, *macushlah,* but the croppies of South America? One fight's good as another, and didn't we have plenty? Grand bloody ones they were. And Bolívar the only honest man of the lot, as it turned out. Spent his own fortune, died without taking a penny for his pains. That's more, begod, than you can say for the *presidentes* and *generales* all scrambling afterwards to line their pockets. And stand each other in front of a firing squad. Republics, did he want? The poor man hasn't stopped spinning in his grave.

"El Dorado?" Blazer shrugged. "Now, I'll tell you it's no worse than some, and better than most. It's not much of a glorious republic, but it rubs along. Here, at least, the honest fellows outnumber the thieves. It suits me well enough. Och, I thought of pulling up stakes when my woman died, it took that much of the heart out of me. But I had my boat and the river trade by then, and gone too old and set in my ways."

Blazer was thoughtful a moment. "The sweet girl was a princess, you know. Princess born, but a queen by nature."

Vesper sat drinking all this in. Despite her usually lucid

perceptions, the dear child has a romantic strain that resists any amount of reasoning. This was, in any case, hardly the moment to point out that the old rogue was spinning preposterous yarns. He might well have fought for Bolívar, as he no doubt would have fought for anything at the drop of a hat. As for his princess—next, he would claim descent from King Brian Boru.

"Full-blooded Chirica, she was," continued Blazer, "a beauty you'll not find again in this world. I'm not one to say it, but I was still a good-looking sort of fellow in those days. A match for any princess, and why not? I've the blood of Brian Boru himself in my veins."

Vesper remained entranced. Captain O'Hara might have held forth longer, but Smiler—or Slider—said something in his ear. He suddenly broke off. His eyes flashed and he thrust his face close to Vesper's.

"De Rochefort? What are the pair of you up to with that scoundrel? You're in it all together, I'll be bound."

"We're not up to anything with him," Vesper calmly replied. "What he may be up to with us, I expect we'll find out when we meet him."

She looked squarely at Blazer as she spoke. "Another thing," she added pleasantly. "You don't have to point your jaw at me. Whatever's on your mind, just come straight out with it. I don't much like being told I'm in something when I don't know what it is."

Blazer locked glances with her for a long moment and finally grinned at her.

"I think you've enough grit in you for a girl and a half, *macushlah.* You'll not want to be mixed up with a fellow like de Rochefort."

"You called him a scoundrel," said Vesper. "I'd like to know why."

"Because he is!" Blazer burst out. "He'd ride roughshod over his old granny for a couple of pesetas. Not just him, there's others, but he's the one doing their dirty work and planning it all out. What else would you call him but a scoundrel? The Chiricas might have a few more names for him."

"The tribe upriver?" asked Vesper. "What's he have to do with them?"

"Do?" Blazer struck the table with his fist. "Do? If he has his way, there'll be none left. To begin with, he means to drown them."

CHAPTER

"I don't understand," said Vesper. "One man can't drown a whole tribe. In the first place, why should he want to?"

"He's going to dig a great bloody ditch," retorted Blazer, "straight across country from sea to sea. The Chiricas are smack in his way. But that's none of his worry. He'll turn their land into a lake bed, and themselves at the bottom of it, village and all."

"He may try building a canal," said Vesper, trying to calm the angry captain, "but how far he'll go with it is something else again. He's not the first to try. From what I've read, the conquistadores wanted a canal, too. They had to give up on it." She turned to me. "Isn't that right, Brinnie?"

When Vesper asks if she is right, she has already decided that she is. There had, in fact, been a number of attempts, over the years, at various sites throughout the isthmus. They had all failed, the schemes abandoned and forgotten. The recent triumph of Monsieur de Lesseps in Suez had no doubt inspired this latest group of impractical speculators. Conditions in El Dorado, however, were altogether different from those in Suez. Here, builders would have to contend with impenetrable jungles, the possibility of earthquakes, a forbidding climate, and countless technical problems beyond the grasp of anyone but a civil engineer.

In view of those difficulties, Vesper and I tried to assure Captain O'Hara that a canal was frankly impossible.

"Then I'll tell you this"—Blazer squinted at us from under his tangled eyebrows—"de Rochefort was one of that Frenchie's chief engineers in Suez. There's talk he's shipping in all manner of newfangled machines. That villain's as clever as they come. If anyone can pull it off, he's the one to do it."

"Even so," said Vesper, "the government will have something to say about it, won't they?"

"The government's for it." Blazer grimaced. "Why shouldn't they be? They got a good fat fee for the construction licenses. They'll have a share of the toll from every ship that passes through."

Vesper did not immediately reply, but sat frowning thoughtfully. I expressed my own opinion: If, by remotest chance, the enterprise proved successful, it would be an excellent source of wealth for El Dorado.

"Except the Chiricas," said Vesper.

"And everyone else," added Blazer. "By the time a few *ministros* and *comisarios* and *funcionarios* get their fingers into the cashbox you'll not see much left over for the rest of El Dorado."

Here, I had to disagree. The profits would be large. Even allowing for a certain amount of peculation—

"Barefaced thievery," muttered O'Hara.

Even at that, I continued, the existence of such a canal would make El Dorado a leader of all Central American countries, and, certainly, the most important shipping center in the hemisphere. El Dorado would enjoy a position of prestige and power among the nations of the world. I saw only benefits.

"Do you?" Blazer glared at me. "You tell me, then, mister professor, where's it carved in stone we need to lead anyone? Position of power? The only position you'll see is one rogue with his hands around another one's throat, and both after a bigger piece of it. We're small potatoes here, and I say that's no sin, is it? We'll manage in our own way, without chewing up half the country."

"You're still forgetting the Chiricas," Vesper insisted.

"Dear girl," I said, "how many can there be? A few hundred? They can be encouraged to move to some other quite attractive corner and be all the better for it."

"Would they?" The glint in Vesper's bright green eyes made it clear she had adopted these obscure *indios* as her personal concern. "They've been there a thousand years and more. Encouraged to move? Booted out is more like it. Dear Brinnie, what a fuss you kicked up when you moved from Clifton Heights to Strafford. Even though," she added wickedly, "you were all the better for it."

I said nothing. The dear girl can sometimes be a shade exasperating, especially when she is being logical.

"Those Chiricas are the only tribe the conquistadores couldn't destroy," said O'Hara. "I know them, I've lived with them. They won't be moved for the sake of a ditch. That's sacred land to them. They've got their ancestors buried there. Ocotalpa's one of their old gods—they don't pay it much mind now, but they used to. It's part of their history, as much as that bell of yours with a great crack in it. There's a sacred lake, too—"

"Matasombra?" put in Vesper.

"Eh?" Blazer cocked an eye. "So it is. How do you know of that? There's a lot I'm beginning to wonder about you."

"One thing you needn't wonder about," said Vesper. "Something can be done. And will be. The Chiricas won't be drowned out, rooted out, or anything else. I'll see to that."

"You'll see to that?" Blazer threw back his head and laughed until the tears started. "*Mavourneen,* aren't you the one! You're cheekier than myself when I was a lad. Here you sit, cool as a cucumber, talking as if you owned the place."

Vesper smiled at him. "I do. All of it."

Vesper had never observed an Irishman at a loss for words, nor had I. It was an awesome sight. Blazer's mouth fell open as if his jaw had suddenly become unhinged; his eyes stared at her. The faces of Smiler and Slider were unblinking as twin moons.

Adelita was the first to speak.

"Peanut for Adelita?" she said. *"Erin go bragh."*

Blazer finally recovered himself. "Get on with you. Here's no matter for joking."

To Vesper's assurances, I added my own. A large man, Blazer required a great amount of convincing. Having listened to all the details Vesper could provide, he rubbed his crust of beard for some while. Then he nodded brusquely.

"All right, then. If what you're saying is true—and for argument's sake I'll grant it may be—there's one best thing you can do. Turn around and sail home."

"We will," said Vesper.

"Good." Blazer nodded in satisfaction.

"Once I've settled whatever needs settling."

"Settle?" cried Blazer. "It's a bad piece of business. Stay out of it."

"I can't stay out of it," said Vesper. "After all, it's my property. I'll clear things up with de Rochefort. In fact, I'll want you on hand when I see him."

Blazer shook his head. "The twins and I sail upriver in an hour. We'll not be in Puerto Palmas again for, what, it could be a fortnight."

"You send me word as soon as you're back," said Vesper. "I won't do anything before I talk to you."

Without awaiting further comment from O'Hara, Vesper tipped her hat over one eye and I followed her out of the cantina, leaving the captain muttering to himself.

Among the many facets of Vesper's remarkable mind is her ability to set aside all other questions and bring her attention to bear intensely on one. In this case, her supper. It was ready for us moments after we arrived at our suite; it was quite acceptable, well served by the entire staff of waiters, and Vesper left not a morsel.

Later, I hoped that she would discuss her plans. She had already committed us to stay in Puerto Palmas for a period much longer than I had calculated. I would have been glad to know exactly what in the world she had been thinking of when she so confidently assured Blazer that she would settle the question of the *indios.*

"I can tell you that, Brinnie. Right now, not the slightest idea. But I expect I'll have one."

CHAPTER 5

Next morning, we met de Rochefort.

The proprietor came to announce that our host awaited us.

"And we've been awaiting him," said Vesper, as the hotelkeeper ushered in that hitherto elusive individual.

If Vesper had formed any picture of him in advance, she had not revealed it to me. Whatever my own expectations as to his age and appearance, Alain de Rochefort no way matched them. I was, in fact, agreeably surprised.

Before us stood a tall, slender young man, a wide-brimmed planter's hat in one hand and in the other a bouquet. The tailoring of his spotless white jacket, the handsomely tooled leather boots, gave him a certain military bearing—he later told us he once served in the Corps du Génie, the renowned French army engineering corps—as well as the air of being equally comfortable in a saddle or a salon chair.

Though his face was sunswept it still showed hints of an

originally fair complexion; he had the light hair, pale eyes, and sharp features found so often among the old French aristocracy. He was, in sum, as engaging and presentable as any Philadelphian.

"Monsieur." He bowed formally. "Mademoiselle Holly. I regret having been so long deprived of the pleasure of meeting you." He offered Vesper the flowers, then delicately raised her hand to his lips.

Vesper has had her hand kissed by royalty, so the gesture could have made no great impression on her. Yet, no doubt, it is a courtesy young women for some reason find pleasant, whatever the source. Not that Vesper blushed or simpered. Vesper has, to my certain knowledge, seldom blushed and never simpered. She smiled openly at him, thanked him for the flowers, and offered him a mango.

"I require no sustenance," de Rochefort answered. "The presence of such a charming young lady is sufficient." He laid a hand on the breast of his jacket. "*Pour toute nourriture, il apporte son coeur*—'for nourishment, he brings only his heart,' as our poet de Musset so beautifully expresses it."

"Didn't he write that about a pelican?" replied Vesper.

"Ah—quite so." For a fraction of a second, de Rochefort seemed taken aback by Vesper's acquaintance with French verse. "But he applied it to himself, as well. In legend, the pelican sacrifices its own lifeblood to feed its offspring. As do all poets, *mademoiselle.*"

"Speaking of pelicans," said Vesper, plainly having no wish to continue a conversation on versifiers or waterfowl, "this canal you're building—you must know it runs through my land. Since you didn't explain anything in your telegram, you can explain it now."

"It was my preference and pleasure to speak with you in person," de Rochefort answered. "The remarkable invention of your Mr. Morse has limitations. The style is too laconic—dare I say telegraphic?—to convey subtleties."

"What's subtle about digging straight through Chirican territory and flooding out a whole tribe?"

"You have been badly misinformed," said de Rochefort. "The situation is not entirely as you describe it."

"That's how Captain O'Hara describes it. We met him yesterday in a cantina—"

De Rochefort laughed lightly. "Where one usually finds him. Old Blazer? Yes, I should have guessed. Poor fellow, I pity him. He is quite deranged, of course. One of our colorful local eccentrics. He is harmless, but there is no grain of truth in him."

"You say he's a liar?"

"No, I accuse him only of an effervescent imagination. And cunning enough to look after his own interests. Once our canal is completed—this grand highway of water, open to newer, larger vessels—his antiquated riverboat will cease to be useful."

"It sounds like you're putting him out of business along with the Chiricas," Vesper said.

"Do you believe that I and my employers are so heartless?" De Rochefort gave Vesper a wounded look. "It is true, his trade will be finished. To make up for that, we have offered him a substantial sum, far more than he could hope to earn if he plied the Culebra for years to come. We have proposed, in effect, to make a rich man of him.

"But, evidently, that does not satisfy him," went on de Rochefort. "It is clear to me that he hopes to extract still more by playing on your sympathies—which, I see, are both noble and abundant. There is, I fear, no limit to human greed."

"What about the tribe of Chiricas?"

"Tribe?" De Rochefort lifted his eyebrows. "Hardly a tribe. A small, scattered handful of the most backward savages, ignorant and superstitious."

"They won't like drowning any more than you would."

"Of course not. Even for these primitives, we wish the best accommodation. That, Mademoiselle Holly, is one reason your presence is necessary. I wish to confer with you on this matter and solicit your opinion."

"What's the other reason?"

"To reach an agreement regarding your land. Yes, I know very well it belongs to you. On behalf of my principals, I have the authority to offer you an excellent price for outright sale; or, if you prefer, you may choose to lease it to us on terms highly favorable to you."

"Suppose I'm not interested either way?"

"Mademoiselle Holly," replied de Rochefort, "we could easily have gone ahead without consulting you, even without your knowledge, and presented you with an accomplished fact. That would have been not only illegal in the technical sense, but dishonorable in the moral sense."

"I don't see where your canal has much to do with honor."

"For me, yes. *L'honneur*—the word means much more in my language than in yours: principle, noblesse, pride."

"Come down to it," said Vesper. "What do you want?"

"All I ask is for you to see with your own eyes exactly what we intend, to examine our plans, our surveys, our financial records. Nothing will be done without your complete approval."

"Nothing?" said Vesper.

"Once you are aware of the facts—as opposed to the figments of Captain O'Hara's imagination—all decisions will be up to your own intelligent judgment.

"But we must act promptly," de Rochefort added. "The rainy season begins in less than three months. Construction must be well under way before that. Allow me, Mademoiselle Holly, to offer you a short visit to our work site. It will be, I assure you, instructive and pleasurable."

Having listened closely to de Rochefort's proposal, I could only be impressed by the young engineer's frankness and completely reasonable attitude. Vesper obviously shared my opinion, for she agreed to let him conduct us on a tour of inspection.

Gallantly offering Vesper his arm, de Rochefort escorted us to the plaza. An elegant open-sided carriage and driver awaited us. This vehicle was drawn not by burros but by a handsome matched pair of horses. De Rochefort helped us to climb in, lithely sprang up to sit beside Vesper, and we set off at a brisk pace.

We headed, first, in the direction of the port but soon turned off and reached the edge of Puerto Palmas. The port was hardly a beehive of activity, but here was a bustling work camp of construction sheds, tents for the labor crews, and a line of railroad track.

Here, de Rochefort told us, he had established a necessary railhead. Owing to natural obstacles, varying depths, and risky navigation, river transportation would be too slow and difficult for the heavy equipment. This would be moved by flatcar. He waved a hand toward a pyramid of wooden crates.

"These hold the components of our bucket dredge, our most effective piece of machinery, specially designed for our purposes. It will be assembled where we propose to begin our excavations."

Caught up in his subject, de Rochefort, with justifiable pride, went on to explain his methods, touching on the advantages of starting in the middle of the canal and extending construction simultaneously east and west. Vesper inquired about any difference in sea levels at the coastlines.

"I have taken all into account," replied de Rochefort, delighted at the opportunity to elaborate on his plans to such a receptive mentality as Vesper's. He went on in detail concerning the nature of canal locks, tributary waterways, dams, and floodgates. Vesper listened intently, interrupting him from time to time with astute questions. De Rochefort answered them fully. And, no doubt, brilliantly. After a certain point, I confess my attention wandered.

"Your eyes are glazing over, Brinnie," observed Vesper. "You'll need an early siesta."

"Forgive me," the attentive de Rochefort quickly put in. "The presence of Mademoiselle Holly has absorbed my interest at the expense of your comfort." He then proposed a cold buffet and liquid refreshment.

"I assume you will take us back to the hotel," I said.

"Our hotel is here," said de Rochefort. "You shall enjoy your luncheon *en voyage.*"

He led us a little way down the rail line to a steam locomotive with one car coupled to it, and assisted us in mounting the steps.

"Better than all our rooms put together," exclaimed Vesper as she entered. Indeed, this railroad carriage compared favorably with the most luxurious Philadelphia drawing room. A brightly patterned Turkey carpet covered the floor. Deep-cushioned armchairs, a dining table, writing desk, mirrored wardrobe, and a potted aspidistra constituted only a few of the lavish appointments. In the ceiling, the blades of a fan rotated steadily, the windows closed to retain the coolness. Discreetly positioned near one of the armchairs was a heavy, polished brass *escupidera*—a word of more gentility than our *spittoon.* In short, no modern convenience had been overlooked.

"A quick journey to the interior, a brief reconnoiter, and then we shall return," said de Rochefort. "Perhaps an hour at most. Hardly time for a civilized *déjeuner,* but we are, after all, in the jungle and must make the best of such hardships."

Excusing himself, telling Vesper he would rejoin us momentarily, de Rochefort sprang down from the car and strode toward the locomotive. I sank gratefully into an armchair.

With a sense of relief, I remarked to Vesper that we could not have been treated with more courtesy and consideration. The magnitude of the business was, I admitted, far greater than I first supposed. Thankfully, Monsieur de Rochefort had shown every sign of bowing to her wishes in what could otherwise have been difficult and lengthy negotiations. His explanations had been most enlightening.

"Yes," Vesper said. "If you assume Blazer's crazy and a greedy liar."

Tropical climates, I suggested, were notorious for producing such effects. Further, we knew nothing of O'Hara beyond what he himself told us. Smiler and Slider were wanted criminals; an honest man would not likely choose such associates.

"I like the twins," Vesper said. "I was just beginning to tell them apart. One's a little bouncier than the other, but I'm not sure which it is. Blazer— I like him, too. And Adelita.

"De Rochefort, with his pelicans and his *honneur*—so far, we don't know anything beyond what *he's* told us."

In my opinion, the young de Rochefort had been quite charmed by Vesper; he would, certainly, be completely candid with her. He was, after all, a gentleman of obvious culture and taste.

Vesper did not reply. That instant, with much hissing of steam, the engine labored into motion. Vesper pressed her nose to the window. Little by little, the mighty locomotive gained momentum and soon was lurching over the track bed at what could have been thirty miles to the hour.

The jungle had been cleared a short distance on either side of the rail line. As we careened along, I had only the impression of plunging through an endless green tunnel; the ropelike lianas, broad-leaved creepers, and dense shrubbery little more than a blur.

Vesper continued to direct her gaze out the window, fascinated by this sheer abundance of vegetation. The car swayed and rocked, not at all disagreeably. I gratefully closed my eyes for a few moments.

Vesper nudged me awake. "Where's de Rochefort?"

I blinked, slightly befuddled by the dear girl rousing me so abruptly from a pleasant sleep. Our host, I answered, must still be in the cab of the locomotive, no doubt giving instructions to the engine driver.

"Another question," said Vesper. "Where's lunch?"

I urged her to be patient, we would not starve to death.

"I mean," said Vesper, "where will it come from? There's a galley, a pantry—but no provisions. De Rochefort's up ahead in the cab, but we can't reach him. I tried. All the doors are locked."

CHAPTER 6

"Of course the doors are locked," I replied, adding that we should appreciate Monsieur de Rochefort's attention to every nicety. Responsible for our well-being, he had taken the precaution of securing the car to assure our complete protection.

As for luncheon, the galley would not be stocked with food sure to spoil in this climate. I envisioned our being provided with an excellent picnic hamper, soon forthcoming. De Rochefort had promised to rejoin us momentarily.

"Momentarily?" returned Vesper. "A devilish long moment. Brinnie, don't you realize? You've been snoozing more than an hour."

By now, I was fully awake and fully puzzled. De Rochefort had indicated no more than one hour for the entire excursion. Yet the train continued its progress, leaving Puerto Palmas far behind. There was a reasonable explanation, I told Vesper, though at present I hesitated to guess what it might be.

"One more question." Vesper had returned to the window and was peering out intently. "Who are those fellows with guns?"

Her words brought me promptly out of my armchair. The train had slowed, the iron wheels grinding to a stop. The cleared area where at last the engine halted was a site much like the one in Puerto Palmas, with its sheds and stores of equipment.

Rifles in hand and cartridge belts slung across their chests, several rough-clad men had begun to approach the locomotive.

I heaved a sigh of relief. They were not bandits, as I first feared, but de Rochefort's employees. Naturally, they would be well armed to guard the work site. De Rochefort had spoken of the Chiricas as savage and superstitious. They might be dangerously hostile as well, if they had come to perceive the canal project as a threat.

"There's de Rochefort," said Vesper. "What's he want with a pistol?"

Our host had jumped down from the cab. He had buckled on a belt and holster. There was no evidence of a picnic hamper. Instead of rejoining us, he strode toward the guards. He had drawn his revolver and, glancing over his shoulder, waved this weapon in our direction. Though his words were inaudible, his gestures made it plain that he was ordering his people to enter our carriage.

I experienced a sense of uneasiness. I could not imagine what they intended, unless to escort us further into the interior.

"Don't wait to find out." Vesper struggled to open the window. "They aren't the board of directors."

Their expressions, I agreed, were stern if not outright unfriendly. Vesper gave a cry of exasperation.

"Sealed tight!"

She ran to another window. I hurried to assist her, but our combined efforts could not raise it. Vesper flung herself away and looked hastily around.

"Brinnie, stand back!"

Vesper's eye had fallen on the heavy brass *escupidera.* She seized this hygienic convenience in both hands and raised it above her head.

I urged her to be careful. We should not damage a private railcar.

Vesper heaved the object with vigor and accuracy. The glass shattered as the *escupidera* burst through the pane like a brass cannonball.

A moment later, we followed it, as Vesper kicked away shards of glass from the frame and sprang through the window. De Rochefort and what I now had to consider his crew of ruffians had just entered the car. Glimpsing me clambering after Vesper, he shouted for us to halt.

Ignoring his command, I dropped heavily beside the track. Vesper helped me up and, without a backward glance, we made for the undergrowth. Any lingering doubts in my mind were dispelled by a volley of rifle fire.

Vesper pitched headlong into the vegetation. I plunged after her, clutching my sun helmet. After the bright sunshine in the clearing, the deep green shadows swallowed us up and nearly blinded us. It took some moments to accustom our eyes to the sudden gloom. Dank air filled my lungs, the overpowering scent of mold, of decomposing foliage caught in my throat. Another rattling volley ripped through the leafy curtain. Even at the risk of losing ourselves in this trackless forest, continued flight in all haste was in our best and immediate interest.

By natural endowment and athletic exercise, Vesper is remarkably fleet of foot. Here, this agility did not serve. Lianas clutched at us, we sank into layers of loamy soil and stumbled over grotesquely twisted roots. The dear girl's face was soon smudged and sweated, she was as nearly winded as I. She had, at least, retained her hat.

She motioned for us to press on nevertheless. "Hard going for them, too. Unless they get machetes and cut their way after us."

Vesper pushed ahead, half-crouched where nets of vines made upright progress impossible. I could not judge by sound how close our pursuers might be. Our passage seemed to rouse every bird in the vicinity, as well as a troop of monkeys, and their indignant screeching practically deafened us. De Rochefort, I feared, could track us by simply following the disturbance.

We persisted through this sweltering maze until even Vesper was obliged to stop and catch her breath. By then, I had begun to hope we had outdistanced our abductor and his henchmen.

"They won't quit," said Vesper. "If de Rochefort went to all the trouble of getting us here, he's not going to let us just slip away."

That was unfortunately true. His deceitful conduct had been shocking. For a military officer of possibly aristocratic forebears, who claimed to set much store in honor and noblesse, such behavior was incomprehensible.

"I don't comprehend it either," admitted Vesper. "I knew he was after something. I still don't know what."

In that, at least, I replied that his motives were all too clear. He wished to eliminate us. Thus, he would also eliminate the inconvenience of Vesper's title to property essential to his project.

"Maybe," said Vesper. "I keep thinking there's more."

"Dear girl, what more could there be?" I reminded her that she possessed one of the world's most valuable pieces of real estate.

"I don't know," said Vesper. "Even if he kills me, he must realize my property goes to my heirs. He won't be able to get his hands on it. I'd guess he has something else up his sleeve. Sooner or later, I'll figure out what it is. Assuming," she added, "we manage to stay alive."

Vesper mopped her face with the bandana from her hat and climbed to her feet. We set off again, sometimes breaking free of the lush growth to cross stretches of scrub. Here, we moved more quickly, but these open areas left us visible to any pursuers as well as exposed to the relentless sun. We had, so far, made good our escape. We still had no idea where we were.

"I worked that out," said Vesper. "Think back. We jumped out the window on the left side of the car. We ran straight into the jungle—"

I broke in to remind her that we had no landmarks. We could have gone in a circle. We could even now be heading toward the rail line.

Vesper shook her head. "I've been keeping an eye on the sun whenever I've a chance. We've been going west for most of the time."

The sun had, in fact, been declining in the same direction as our path. I would have made the same observation had my thoughts not been otherwise occupied.

"If we keep going," Vesper went on, "sooner or later we have to reach the Culebra. Once we do that, we follow it to Puerto Palmas."

This, in theory, was correct. It did not take into account the difficulties of thrashing our way through miles of jungle.

"I'd rather go thrashing," replied Vesper. "It's better than sitting waiting for de Rochefort to find us."

Tropical nightfall comes abruptly, for which I was thankful. De Rochefort would be unable to continue his search. By the same token, we did not dare to keep up our flight. While we still could see, I suggested finding a suitable hiding place until morning.

Vesper agreed, and we trampled out a nest in the undergrowth. The dear girl dropped off to sleep immediately. The orchestra of tree frogs, insects, and the weird cries of night creatures actually seemed to soothe her. For myself, the prospect of being set upon by *tigres*—as jungle felines in general were called in this part of the world—did not trouble me. I was certain that no predator would attack us deliberately. However, the mosquitoes had already discovered me.

We started again at first light and continued several hours, Vesper trudging a little ahead of me.

"Here's the Culebra," she called out.

She had halted just beyond a curtain of high, reedlike plants. There was no expanse of beach. The brownish water flowed almost at our feet, gently curving and sun-speckled, a liquid snakeskin.

Vesper stood gazing at the opposite shore. At this point the Rio Culebra was wider than some reaches of our majestic Delaware River. "I'd feel better if we had this between us and de Rochefort."

So would I, but saw no way to achieve that. Vesper is a strong swimmer, but I could not permit her to test her skill against the Culebra—even setting aside the possibility of caymans and other water reptiles.

"All right, we won't try swimming," Vesper said. "Not here, anyway. Float across? I guess we could put together some sort of raft. Still, we'd be sitting ducks—or drifting ducks—for de Rochefort."

She decided, then, to continue on foot downstream until we found a more likely crossing.

"We have to go that way anyhow," said Vesper, striking off again through the undergrowth. "We know where we are now."

After another hour or so, the Culebra did turn a little shallower, with a narrow apron of shoreline. Vesper hurried to investigate, then halted in her tracks and signaled me to silence. The foliage had kept us from seeing the figure of a man at the water's edge.

It was too late. He had heard us approaching. He turned quickly to face us, a length of rope in his hands.

CHAPTER 7

Vesper gave a glad cry and ran to him. "Slider! That's you, isn't it?"

"It is, miss. And that's you!" The twin popped his eyes at Vesper. "I can't say I thought we'd run into you. Or, put it that you'd run into us." Slider's quick glance took in our disheveled appearance. "What's happened to you?"

"I'll tell you later," said Vesper. "Where's Blazer? And Smiler?"

"Aboard the *Libertador.* As things are going, or not going, that's likely where we'll stay." Slider beckoned for us to follow him. "She broke down, hardly out of Puerto Palmas—as often happens, we're used to it. We fixed her up and she broke down again. Captain Blazer put in for the night. then our mooring line parted. I've seen to that now, but we're still dead in the water. For how long, I can't say. That's more Smiler's line of work."

Slider led us toward the riverbank. The curtain of trees and shrubbery had kept me from seeing that the Culebra had swung inward to form a cove, a little backwater where

O'Hara had secured his disabled craft. A rickety gangway had been run out, and we clambered over it.

Smiler—or Slider—had called the *Libertador* a trim vessel. She might once have been, in earlier days. Now the stern wheel looked cobbled together from parts of some antique windmill. The smokestack, with a battered crown of ironwork, tilted at much the same angle as Pisa's famous leaning tower. The *Libertador* no way compared to the mighty ships in our port of Philadelphia. Even so, the little riverboat had excellent lines. She was compact, well constructed, and she might still have the ability to make rapid headway—though presently making no headway whatever.

Blazer, shirtless and grimy, had just come stamping above deck. His beard was clotted, his temper likewise. At sight of Vesper, however, his scowl turned to a grin of pleasure and surprise. When Vesper briefly explained our presence, his face fell.

"*Mavourneen,* I told you the fellow was a scoundrel. You should have kept clear of him and the whole dirty business." He motioned for us to climb up to the pilothouse. Adelita, perched on the wheel, cast a wicked eye on me as if she recalled our first encounter. I sat on a bench out of range of her beak while Vesper provided O'Hara with further details.

"Calls me a liar and madman, does he?" cried Blazer after she had finished her account, including her employment of the *escupidera* as the instrument of our escape.

Blazer paced back and forth, as much as this was possible in the confines of the pilothouse. He was outraged and fuming at the attempted kidnapping, and equally so at de Rochefort's slander of him.

"Buy me out? Make a rich man of me? I've done well

in the river trade, and better than well, and come by it without tricks or cheating. Not that I've saved much. I've spent all to good purpose these years. No, he didn't offer me a brass peseta. Squeeze money from you? *Macushlah,* I want nothing of you at all. What I want is an end to his bloody digging, and himself out of El Dorado.

"But that's neither here nor there at this moment," Blazer went on. "The thing is: What will the pair of you do now?"

"Ask you to sail us to Puerto Palmas," Vesper answered without hesitation.

Blazer halted his pacing. "Sweet mercy, why should you even think of going there? That's what the calumniating scoundrel counts on, isn't it? You gave him the slip once, he'll not let it happen again. He'll be after you with blood in his eye. Puerto Palmas? The first place he'll look! You two best drop out of sight and leave things to cool."

"That's what I had in mind," said Vesper. "De Rochefort must think we've headed downriver. What else would we do? So, we'll go upriver. With you, Blazer. If you'll take us on as passengers."

O'Hara rubbed his face with a heavy-knuckled hand. "That—that won't answer too well. I've urgent business, you see."

"What difference does it make?" Vesper persisted. "We won't be in the way. When you're done, we'll go with you to Puerto Palmas. Of course," she added, "the other thing we can do is hide in the jungle."

"I can't let you do that." Blazer blew out a long breath. "All right," he said at last. "You'll stay on the *Libertador.* Keep out of sight, mind you, and keep from underfoot once we're under way. When that may be, I've no idea."

Blazer turned to squint at his gauges, then snatched up the speaking tube. "Smiler, we're not showing as much pressure as I can spit."

"What's wrong?" Vesper asked, as Blazer snorted and flung down the tube.

"If I knew that, I'd mend it," Blazer grumbled. "I'm late with my cargo as it is. If I don't soon deliver my goods, there'll be the very devil to pay."

Blazer would have had us make ourselves comfortable while he went below to the engine room, but Vesper offered to go with him and help.

"You, *mavourneen*? There's no help you can give us. Smiler and I can manage."

Vesper, nevertheless, insisted. O'Hara shrugged skeptically. Vesper stepped down the ladder after him. I doubted that she could provide much assistance. She had, at one time, shown interest in steam power, with a view to designing an improved carriage propelled by that awesome force. I had tried to persuade her the notion was impractical. She had, in any case, turned her inquiring mind to other subjects. Marine engines, I believed, would lie beyond even Vesper's competence.

Meantime, I paced along the hurricane deck, past the officers' quarters: a structure our American boatmen would have called a "texas," though here it hardly qualified for so expansive a term. It was little more than a partitioned shack, a striking contrast to the accommodations on the *City of Brotherly Love.*

Recollection of that splendid vessel only reminded me of our present plight. Once again in Puerto Palmas, our troubles would begin in earnest. We must find and board a ship. De Rochefort would surely have his agents scouring the port. Watching the few outbound vessels and their passengers would present no difficulty for him. Our money, baggage, and papers were in the hotel, we dared not return for them. We could not claim sanctuary in the American embassy or consulate. El Dorado did not enjoy the presence of those august institutions.

As for the local authorities, if they favored the canal project and its chief engineer, they would likely turn a deaf ear to any complaints that might disrupt the work.

Slider soon arrived to break in upon my analysis of our problems. An enormous grin divided his face into half-moons.

"If you could see Miss Vesper! She's got old Blazer and Smiler taking the whole engine apart." He wagged his head in admiration. "She's climbing about like a monkey. I'll lay a wager she'll have us under way."

So I hoped, for it had occurred to me that de Rochefort and his gang would sooner or later come upon the disabled *Libertador.* If he suspected our presence, he would not hesitate to board. As a routine matter, I had included my revolver in our baggage. I cursed myself for not having brought the weapon. My first duty was to protect Vesper in all circumstances. But who would have supposed a short train ride and picnic luncheon would entail a need for firearms?

Slider, on instructions from Captain O'Hara, conducted me to a cubbyhole in the texas. I flung myself into a hammock to pursue my thoughts. Adelita, with almost human perversity, had chosen to perch there.

"Good time, sailor!" the depraved fowl cackled. *"¡Caramba!"*

I ignored her baleful eye. Despite myself, I drifted off for what must have been an hour or so, until roused by an earsplitting racket.

It was not Adelita performing the Battle of Puerto Palmas, though she added her own whoops and shrieks.

Moments later, Vesper burst into the texas. She was begrimed, grease-daubed, her face flushed and triumphant.

"We're moving, Brinnie! Most of the trouble was the steam inlet. Blazer and Smiler hadn't bothered—"

She broke off and hustled me to the deck. The racket that awakened me was the paddlewheel trembling and straining into motion. It was churning the water of the cove while jets of steam spurted like geysers. Blazer, in the pilothouse, had started backing the *Libertador* into the current.

"We'll be fine, now," said Vesper. "If it happens again, I showed them what to do."

Later, once on our way, with Slider and Smiler taking turns at the helm, Blazer treated us to a celebratory supper in his cabin. His spirits had lifted, thanks to Vesper. He hoped to make up for lost time. Barring further setbacks, he would conclude his business and soon return us to port.

"Now, if you could only deal with de Rochefort as easily as you did with our engine," he told Vesper, "you'd do more than earn your passage."

"What I'm trying to understand," replied Vesper, "is why he's building a canal here in the first place."

"Look at the map," said Blazer. "Once he's done on the Culebra, he'll cut into Lake Flores. From there, it's no distance west to the Pacific."

"What I mean," said Vesper, "is why he'd risk it with a volcano in his backyard. I know it's supposed to be extinct, but how can he be sure? And what about earthquakes?"

"He's not worried," said Blazer. "He's had his geologist experts poke and pry all over the site. From what I hear, they've reported no sign of Ocotalpa ever coming to life. Earthquakes? Those science fellows tell him the fault lines run elsewhere. If there's any earthquake, he can be sure it won't harm his canal."

Blazer laughed and slapped the table. "You tickle Ocotalpa to blow off as much steam as you tickled out of my engine and he'll think twice about going on with his ditch. Lay on a good earthquake, too. You can bet he'll shut down the whole business and pull out. Any whiff of danger, he'll be off to bedevil some other country. He's a scoundrel, but he's not a fool.

"You're a girl and a half, *mavourneen*— No, from today I'd say a girl and three-quarters. But eruptions and earthquakes are past your doing."

Vesper nodded. "No way that I can see."

This was one of the rare times the dear girl had made such an admission. Usually, she had no lack of confidence in her capabilities. Then she added, "Not at the moment, anyhow."

Blazer left us, then, to relieve Smiler—or Slider—in the pilothouse. As Vesper and I made our way to our quarters, she lingered by the rail. She gazed down at the river. There was the shadow of a frown on her face, an air of concentration, as if she were still chewing over the last of her supper.

For a moment, the alarming notion struck me that she might actually be pondering some challenge to Ocotalpa. To my relief, she was not.

"Blazer's cargo," she said. "When I finished in the engine room, and they were cleaning up, I took a peek into the hold. Blazer's carrying a lot of goods."

I supposed so. There would naturally be a brisk demand for hand tools, pots and pans, and similar domestic merchandise.

"You're only half-right," said Vesper. "There's plenty of merchandise. Rifles and ammunition."

CHAPTER 8

"Not that it's any of our business," Vesper went on. "Blazer helped us out of a tight spot, he was good-hearted enough to take us along. We're his guests, the *Libertador*'s his home. We've no right prying into his bureau drawers."

To that, I emphatically agreed. If he chose to transport an arsenal of weapons, or a herd of wild elephants, it did not concern us. However, when Vesper admits that something is not her business, she finds a way to make it so.

In this case, she did not. She raised no questions with O'Hara, nor said a word to him about the peculiar nature of his so-called trade goods. She did not even try to pump further information out of Smiler and Slider.

Instead, she fell easily and comfortably into the daily routine of the boat. Blazer, for all his dubious profession, was a first-rate pilot and officer. The twins, whatever had been their shady past, went about their duties with cheerful dispatch. In consequence, Blazer was able to run the *Libertador* with something even less than a skeleton crew.

Vesper eagerly helped. Sometimes she worked with Blazer in the pilothouse, where he occasionally let her take the helm, sometimes with Slider, casting the lead for continual sounding of the river bottom, or with Smiler in the engine room.

Adelita had attached herself to me. Wherever I wandered, above deck or below, she would find and come flapping after me, a gleam in her eyes and a determination to nip. Perhaps it was her way of showing affection.

While Vesper occupied herself with voluntary duties, I tried to foresee a plan of action for us once we returned to Puerto Palmas. But my thoughts led nowhere. The baking sun, the river slipping by, put me in an almost lazy frame of mind.

Enjoying this drowsy idleness one afternoon, I must have suffered a momentary heat stroke. As I gazed shoreward from the rail of the hurricane deck, the distant greenery shimmered before my eyes a fraction of a second. The effect was not unlike that of an earth tremor. I was glad the geologists had established the impossibility of any such harmful event. Then I realized it was simply the weather. Hot climates can play many optical tricks. I went back to admiring the view.

Apart from mosquitoes and furry spiders, *tigres* in the undergrowth, alligators pretending to bask innocently in the shallows, anacondas and other serpents, the Culebra must be one of the most beautiful rivers in the world. Between banks of exotic blossoms, it would curve gracefully along its course, then run straight and deep for miles, or fork around flower-laden islets rising in midstream.

"Imagine what de Rochefort and his bucket dredge will

do to this—not to mention the Chiricas," observed Vesper. "Well, I'll have my say about that. Part of it's mine, after all. But—how can the river belong to anybody but itself?"

In strict sense of ownership, we had not yet reached Vesper's property. Blazer told us that it lay another day upriver. We had, meantime, been passing numbers of small settlements, their wooden piers reaching into the current. They were almost entirely on the west bank and, I presumed, made up the main source of Blazer's business. He stopped at none of them, however, and so far had conducted no trade at all.

The Culebra began to veer sharply south, in the oxbow Vesper had discerned on her map before we left Strafford.

"It's bigger than I expected," she told me. "I see why de Rochefort wants to cut straight across. It makes sense—to him. If he followed the river, the canal would have to go miles out of the way. Blazer meant it when he talked about turning this into a lake. That's just what would happen."

By midmorning next day, we had almost rounded the long curve of the oxbow when the river notched in to form a sheltered harbor. Unlike the steeply rising banks we had been sailing past, here the shore gently sloped in a wide, beachy apron.

Blazer deftly maneuvered the *Libertador* into this inlet, Smiler and Slider ran out the gangway. Vesper, of course, had to be first ashore, pulling me along with her.

Blazer did not blow his whistle or give any other sign of his arrival. The *Libertador,* however, must have been observed by invisible watchers. No sooner had we stopped than some dozen *indios* appeared as if out of nowhere.

"Chiricas," said Vesper. "They must be."

The men hurried aboard, hardly glancing at us. They

were, in stature, somewhat shorter than the average Philadelphian, with the same lustrous eyes and copper skin as the *indios* we observed in Puerto Palmas. But these wore their blue black hair much longer, and cut off sharply a little below their shoulders. They dressed in a version of the *taparrabo,* an item of apparel something between a wide loincloth and a narrow kilt.

"They don't look as savage as de Rochefort told us," Vesper said. "If they're ignorant, they certainly know their way around Blazer's boat."

I withheld judgment on their disposition, but Vesper's observation was well taken. They appeared familiar with the *Libertador* and made their way directly to the cargo hold without need of direction from Smiler or Slider. Soon, more of their fellows joined them. In no time, they formed a human chain, passing crates and chests from hand to hand.

O'Hara was not only selling them firearms, his entire cargo seemed destined exclusively for their use. Frankly, I was appalled.

"What did you suppose?" Vesper said. "I thought that's what Blazer was up to as soon as I saw what he was carrying."

The idea had, in fact, crossed my mind. I had dismissed it, unwilling to believe that even Blazer would be so irresponsible or eager for business that he would arm a simple, primitive folk with dangerous modern weapons.

"They aren't so primitive, Brinnie." Vesper pointed toward a couple of the men who had already broken out rifles from the crates and were very competently examining the firing mechanisms, smartly racking the bolts back and forth and peering down the barrels.

Vesper tugged at my arm. "I think Blazer would be happier if we kept out of the way."

I supposed she meant for us to return aboard. Instead she strode from the shore toward a fringe of palms. Some of the Chiricas, bearing ammunition chests on their heads had already set off briskly in that direction.

"Do they have a village here?" Vesper quickened her pace. "Let's have a look. How many people live there? That's another thing," she added. "De Rochefort made it sound like only a handful skulking around in the jungle."

I had no urgent interest in the size of the local population. Vesper would be far better off in our quarters. I knew nothing of the Chiricas and their ways. While offloading the firearms occupied their attention at the moment, they might rapidly turn curious about our presence. They could, for all I knew, have extremely volatile temperaments. Strangers, in any case, would not likely be welcome witnesses to an unquestionably illegal transaction.

"They'll see we don't mean any harm," Vesper said confidently.

"No doubt," I replied. "I only wonder how long it will take them to realize it."

"Just try not to look so ferocious, Brinnie."

As I continued my efforts to reason with her, she cried out in surprise and stopped in her tracks. We had come face to face with one of the Chiricas making his way toward the riverbank.

He, too, halted, taken aback at the sight of us. He stood nearly a head taller than I, lean and muscular, his skin deeply bronzed, his cheeks and brows streaked with vivid blues and yellows. Unlike those of his fellows, his *taparrabo* was elaborately embroidered and dyed in a rainbow of colors. Around his neck hung an intricately worked ornament of bright feathers.

Young though he was—he could scarcely have reached his middle twenties—there was no question in my mind. We were in the presence of no less a personage than the tribal chieftain himself. I based my conclusion not only on the splendor of his attire but as much on his bearing. His posture, the carriage of his head, his air of complete self-assurance conveyed the same calm authority as that of our oldest Philadelphia families. Like theirs, his facial expression was not easily read.

Uncertain of his intentions, I stepped protectively in front of Vesper. Raising my sun helmet, giving every indication of respect and good will, I spoke in carefully enunciated tones.

"Professor." I pointed to myself. "Professor Brinton Garrett."

He made a similar gesture. "Acharro."

Unfamiliar with the Chirican dialect, I addressed him in Nahuatl. He gazed steadily but without comprehension. I ventured to employ my smattering of Quechuan. He folded his arms and glanced at me with bemusement.

I resorted now to sign language, trying to express the idea that we had arrived by water from a great city far to the north, a place of many people and high buildings. Acharro frowned and shook his head.

"Try English," he said. "We might understand each other better. Or do you wish to tell me that you live in an anthill?"

CHAPTER 9

Vesper would not have remained speechless for long even if one of the local jaguars padded up and addressed her in classical Greek. While I stood too dumbstruck to reply in any language at all, she stepped past me, introduced us, and made a courteous apology on my behalf.

Acharro, his arms still folded, studied Vesper for some long moments. He turned again to me.

"Your mistake is understandable. You find yourself in a remote jungle, amid a tribe of savages. You make certain assumptions about them, forming your opinions in advance, based on your previous experience and what you consider to be logical. Your error, as I said, is quite understandable. It is, however, not excusable."

I thought it time for us to get back to the *Libertador*. Acharro was very much a chieftain, but he was also a very prickly sort of fellow, and he had begun making me uncomfortable. Vesper, though, had caught his interest, and he was not inclined to let us go quietly on our way. Our presence aboard the riverboat did not especially please him.

"Have you come to observe us," he demanded of Vesper, "to conduct an investigation of our primitive manners and customs—before we are entirely extinct?"

"Acharro," Vesper said sweetly, looking him squarely between the eyes, "you're making assumptions, forming your opinion in advance. That's perfectly understandable." She smiled at him. "I'd say it's also perfectly excusable."

Acharro's jaw went up, his face tightened an instant. He did not reply, but gave some quick instructions to one of the passing Chiricas. He glanced at Vesper, then turned on his heel to stride back along the path.

"I'm assuming we're to follow," said Vesper. "I'll explain it all to him later."

Wait, I said to myself, until the dear girl explains who owns his land and has the papers to prove it. I had a feeling that Vesper's documents would not carry much weight with Acharro.

We went only a little distance from the shore, but the jungle already pressed in. Acharro paced on ahead, lithe and silent as a *tigre.* Before we became aware of it, the village sprang up before us.

Though not exactly fortified, it was well protected by a palisade of slender stakes lashed together with fibers. A spacious central area of hard-packed clay was faced by huts of rattan and woven palm leaves. Some of these structures were dwellings, others given over to workshops of weavers, cloth dyers, pot makers. All were nicely sited along carefully laid out little streets, or *avenidas.*

Most of the men were busy hauling in Blazer's cargo of lethal weapons—an occupation that made something of a jarring contrast with the general atmosphere of innocent rustic activity. The village women, some with infants slung at their hips, pretended not to watch us, but gave us side glances of intense curiosity. They wore skirts much like those of the Puerto Palmas *indias,* although here they seemed much brighter in color. A band of small boys scampered boldly after us, but shied away from following Acharro into the largest of the structures. This building, with a long, low-roofed verandah, I took to be a combination council house and Acharro's own quarters.

He led us to a chamber whose far side was open to the breeze, with a grass curtain that could be raised or lowered. Acharro, in one easy movement, sat himself cross-legged on the floor. Vesper did likewise, while I hunkered down as best I could. Acharro had issued no instructions, but within moments one of the younger women—called "Suncha," as we later learned—arrived with a basket of fruit which she set on the ground and hastily departed.

Vesper gladly investigated these refreshments. Her eye fell on a wickerwork shelf of books and, uninvited, she went to examine them.

"Here's Euclid's geometry," she called out. "And a nice set of Rousseau, and—" She stopped and grinned at him. "All right, Acharro. Yes, I'm really surprised."

Acharro opened his mouth to reply—something prickly, no doubt—but thought better of it. Vesper's earlier rejoinder might have made him a little wary of bandying words with her. Then he actually gave her half a smile.

"Before you speculate, Miss Holly," he said, "I can spare you the effort. I studied for a time at Cambridge University in England. I have been home two years now, and gladly so. From what I have seen of your civilization, I prefer to be among my Chiricas."

If Acharro hoped to astonish Vesper and perhaps even up the score between them, he did not succeed. Vesper, for some perverse reason, has never shown much reverence for institutions of higher learning, including our own University of Pennsylvania.

"Cambridge is a good school," Vesper said, "as schools go. As for our civilization, at least in Philadelphia no one's tried to kidnap me."

"What are you telling me?" demanded Acharro. "Why should anyone in El Dorado wish to kidnap you?"

"I suppose," said Vesper, "it's because of the canal, and because Brinnie and I are here to do something about it."

"To do what?" asked Acharro.

"I don't know yet," Vesper said. "You see, the way it started—"

A raucous yell interrupted her. Adelita had come flapping in, and the impudent fowl made straight to perch on my head. Blazer followed, Acharro stood up and the two held out their arms in what I presumed was a Chirican *abrazo* or some other sort of ritual embrace.

"You've met my passengers, then," Blazer said to Acharro when this small ceremony was completed. "They've had a nasty run-in with de Rochefort. I'm taking them under my wing for a time." He nodded toward Vesper. "Without the sweet colleen here, I'd have been even later."

I remarked to Blazer that the pleasure of meeting Acharro had been all ours, though it had begun on a note of misunderstanding. I added, with a courteous nod to

Acharro, that I had neglected to compliment him on his excellent English, which he spoke with remarkable fluency.

"And why shouldn't he?" said Blazer. "The lad's my son. Do you think I'd have him grow up ignorant as his old dad?"

CHAPTER

"Didn't it nearly break my heart and my purse, sending him to the English? They give good schooling, no matter. So I let bygones be bygones—that far, anyway.

" 'Acharro,' " Blazer went on. "That's Chirica for 'O'Hara.' I called the lad 'Boylan Bolívar '; his dear mother called him 'Machico.' 'Acharro's' what stuck, though, after they named him chief."

"I am my father's son and my mother's child," Acharro said, glancing at Blazer with affection, "whatever name I bear."

As I studied the young man, I detected a vague similarity of features, though Acharro probably took more after his mother than the rough and ready Blazer. I should have suspected. Had his face not been daubed with all that paint, I might sooner have noticed the blue eyes hardly characteristic of the Chiricas.

"Boylan Bolívar Machico O'Hara Acharro?" said Vesper, not all that much taken aback by the revelation. She would have shown the same cordial interest if Blazer had claimed to be the nephew of Benjamin Franklin. "That's nice. It should make things pleasanter—all in the family."

"We'll stand by each other, if that's what you mean," said Blazer. "For the rest—"

"The rest is what I want to talk about," said Vesper. "Starting with those rifles."

"Ah, them," said Blazer. "I'm sorry about them."

"I should hope so," Vesper said.

"Sorry, they're all I could lay hands on," Blazer said to Acharro. "I'll go back for one more shipment, and that's the last. The last of my money, too."

"What are you doing with them in the fiist place?" Vesper said, adding, "I've a pretty good idea."

"Then you have no reason to ask," Acharro said. "In any event, it is not your concern."

"I think it is," replied Vesper. "I like to know what's going on in my property."

Acharro, despite his efforts, could not hide his surprise as he listened to Vesper's account. At last, he regained his composure. His features turned stony, his expression impossible to read. I doubted that he was happy.

"You call this land yours?" he said. "Until now, you knew nothing of its existence. It is yours only because the law says it is."

"That's a place to start," said Vesper.

"Is it?" replied Acharro. "The law may be on your side. It is not on ours. When I learned of the canal that will destroy my Chiricas, I myself went to the *residencia* in Puerto Palmas."

"Where they treated you like a savage," I burst out,

unable to keep down my indignation. Acharro, after all, was a university man.

"I did not go dressed in this." Acharro pointed to his *taparrabo.* "I did them the courtesy of wearing their costume. No, they did not treat me like a savage. They treated me like a fool.

"I asked them to leave us in peace, to find some other course for their canal. We are the last of our kind, and I asked them not to destroy our sacred home. If they did, they would be acting like the conquistadores they overthrew.

"They asked one question of me: How much could my Chiricas add to the national treasury? They knew the answer as well as I did—nothing. They took a sheet of paper and drew a picture for me, as if I were a child unable to read —on one side, the profits from the canal, on the other, the profits from my Chiricas. They had no more to say. I understood, then, what must be done.

"In the old days, we would have called on Ocotalpa to rise up against our enemies. We would have summoned the spirits of Lake Matasombra to stand by our side, the Great Cayman from the river, and the Black Jaguar."

Acharro's voice had taken a different tone. He spoke in deep, rolling cadences. His eyes held a blue fire, the streaks of paint over his wide cheekbones seemed to glow. Vesper, silent, watched him with a peculiar expression on her face. The dear girl might have been uneasy, for I felt my own skin prickle and the hairs twitch on my neck. Had I been a Chirica, I would have been awed. Luckily, I am a Philadelphian.

Acharro had almost convinced me these ancient spirits

lived—or that he fervently believed they did. Then he broke off, a wry smile on his lips.

"I did not call on Ocotalpa and the Black Jaguar. They are unreliable. I asked my father to buy guns."

"And Blazer's ruined himself getting them," said Vesper, after a moment when the spell had broken. "You'll ruin yourselves using them. Who will you fight? The work crews? De Rochefort will bring more. Comes to that, the government will send in troops, the whole army if they have to. Leave you in peace? I suppose they will. Most of you will be dead."

"I am aware of that," said Acharro. "My Chiricas—"

"You keep talking about your Chiricas," Vesper said. "They don't belong to you, you belong to them. 'When a man assumes public trust, he should consider himself as public property.' "

"Do not quote your Thomas Jefferson at me," retorted Acharro. "We no longer have a king. I am a chief by my tribe's consent, and indeed public property. I am also responsible for leading them. I have explained our position. It is unlikely that any of us will survive. They accept that, every man."

"And the women?" Vesper demanded. "The children? Did you explain it to them?" She rounded on Blazer. "And you've been helping him. Are you willing for your son to get himself and everybody else killed?"

"I'll be with him," Blazer said. "My time's running out, *macushlah.* What's a better way to go than one last grand and glorious shindy? Give me the chance, I'll take de Rochefort with me."

"Acharro," said Vesper, "you don't think much of civilization. But you're ready to shed blood, as the conquistadores did."

"You forget I am half a savage." Acharro smiled bitterly. "Even savages do not politely let themselves be exterminated."

"I don't care if you're polite or not," returned Vesper. "I don't want you, or anybody, exterminated. What would you say if I told you there's a better way?"

" 'A man says what he knows,' " answered Acharro. " 'A woman says what will please.' "

"Don't quote Rousseau at me," retorted Vesper. "When it comes to women, he's full of beans. I'm not trying to please you, I'm trying to keep all of you alive. What would you say if I could do that? What would you say if I told you I had a plan with a very good chance of working?"

"I would listen," said Acharro. "I am listening now."

"I still have a couple details to figure out."

"Do so, then," ordered Acharro. "Speak with Professor Garrett. When you are ready, I will call a meeting of our council. The professor will offer your plan to them."

"What?" exclaimed Vesper. "Nothing against dear old Brinnie, but I'm capable of offering it myself."

"Women have no voice in our council," replied Acharro. "It is not our custom."

"It isn't our custom, either," said Vesper. "When our women try, our men lock them up in jail, poke a tube down their throats and pour food into them if they won't eat."

"I know that," said Acharro. "It is barbarity. We would not do such a thing."

"We're not as civilized as you are." Vesper smiled at him. "Here's your chance to go us another one better.

Besides, if you don't let me speak up on my own, I won't speak up at all."

Acharro's face turned stormy. "A chieftain is not addressed in this manner."

"I think I just did," said Vesper.

"Think better of it, then." Acharro stood up. With a curt motion of his hand, he indicated that our audience, or whatever it might be called, was over.

Vesper was not ready to be dismissed. Though Blazer expected us to return aboard the *Libertador,* she declined.

"If de Rochefort happens to sight the boat, it's better if Brinnie and I aren't there. I'd rather stay in the village—if Chief Acharro is gracious enough to let us."

Acharro glowered a moment at Vesper. "It is not our custom to refuse hospitality. Suncha will attend you."

"Thank you, Chief Acharro." Vesper gave him a thoroughly wicked glance. "I'd like to know more of your customs."

CHAPTER

11

"Dear girl," I murmured, once we were clear of Acharro's *residencia* and in the charge of Suncha, "you took a terrible risk, stirring him up like that. For all his Cambridge education, he might have handed us our heads."

"I doubt it," said Vesper. "I don't think head-hunting is a Chirican custom. Our heads are perfectly safe. All the more since Acharro thinks there's something useful in mine. I wish there were."

"Good heavens," I cried, "and you told Acharro you had a plan!"

"No," said Vesper. "I only asked him what he'd say if I did."

Acharro, I pointed out, was not in a frame of mind for hairsplitting. I did not like to think of what it would do for his disposition when he found out that Vesper had been splitting hairs very fine indeed.

"He'll be all right. O'Hara-Acharro—" Vesper hesitated an instant. Her voice carried an odd little tone. In ordinary circumstances, I would have called it a note of fondness. Here, obviously, it was simple curiosity.

"I don't think he's decided whether he's a savage playing at being civilized, or a civilized man playing at being a savage," Vesper added. "He may not live to find out."

We crossed the village plaza and followed Suncha down one of the *avenidas.* Near the back palisade, I glimpsed part of an area carefully cleared and flattened. I noticed three short poles upright in the ground. Presumably a Chirican fetish or tribal totem of some kind, but they reminded me oddly of the wicket featured in the British national pastime, cricket.

I had no opportunity to inquire about the significance or magical properties of these totem rods, for Suncha now led us into her dwelling—a very pleasant one, larger than I had expected. She indicated the room we would occupy and told us—in quite acceptable English—that she would obtain hammocks and whatever else we required.

"This is lovely, Suncha," Vesper said, "but we don't want to put you out of your own house."

"My *alcoba* is in the back. This is our schoolroom," Suncha replied. "We have not used it much since—since the trouble began. We are all too busy with other things."

Suncha was a bright-faced, handsome young woman. Though she had been close-lipped and withdrawn in the presence of Acharro, she blossomed noticeably and showed a lively spirit the more Vesper chatted with her. Suncha was, in fact, the village schoolmistress.

"Acharro taught me to read and write, now I teach the others. We study Spanish, English, arithmetic; some history and geography," she told Vesper. "Chirican is not a written language, so Acharro has also ordered me to prepare a dictionary and grammar." Suncha shook her head. "I fear there will be no time to finish."

"There will, if I can manage it," said Vesper.

"I do not think that is possible," Suncha replied. "Acharro has tried all he can."

"He has," Vesper agreed. "I haven't."

Meanwhile, a number of women and children had gradually drifted into the room. They had been shy at our arrival. Now, among themselves, they were curious to examine us at close range.

Vesper's clothing interested them, at first, more than anything else. They gathered around her, fingering the material of her jacket and trousers with an almost professional air.

They were, I supposed, impressed by the quality of such goods.

"No. They say it is very bad. They admire the señorita's hair, the color of our chicha bird's feathers. They are sorry a pretty girl has to wear such poor material."

To demonstrate further, Suncha fetched a basket filled with lengths of cloth. Unfolding the material, Vesper gave a cry of delight.

"Amazing, Brinnie! Done so beautifully—their own fibers, mostly, and some yarns Blazer must have brought."

What caught Vesper's interest, beyond the excellence of the fabric itself, was the woven pattern of figures human and animal spreading across the material. In style, they were not unlike those of the ancient Aztecs or Mayas.

"The design has been handed down to us—from who knows how long ago," Suncha said, as Vesper inquired about it. "This is the Black Jaguar who protects us in the jungle. And this, the River Cayman who guards the supply of fish. Here, the great Ocotalpa, who will rise up in wrath and rain fire on the heads of our foes."

"Did Ocotalpa ever help you?"

Suncha laughed and shook her head. "He rises in wrath when it suits him, not us. Acharro says the conquistadores recorded an eruption when they first came here, another came twenty years later. There have been a few more, from time to time, but none within the memory of any living person. I think Ocotalpa has gone to sleep and will not wake again."

"De Rochefort's counting on that," said Vesper. "So Acharro's counting on his rifles."

Encouraged by Vesper's interest, Suncha displayed some earthenware from her own quarters. These strikingly shaped and painted objects were, indeed, as remarkable as the fabrics. They would have been given pride of place in any museum in the world or even a Philadelphia drawing room.

"Your men do splendid work," I remarked to Suncha. "I should go as far as to call them fine artists."

At this came an outburst of giggling and much laughter behind hands. The sudden merriment puzzled me. I wondered if my compliments had been properly understood.

"This is our work," Suncha explained, "not the men's. The idea of our men doing it is *cómico,* so funny it makes us laugh."

"What do your men do, then?" Vesper asked.

"They are Caymans. Or Jaguars."

These creatures, I told Vesper, would be the animal

emblems of clans or families. My explanation produced further merriment. Since the women had grown more at ease with Vesper, their laughter tended to be franker and louder than before.

"They are cricket teams," said Suncha. "Also, *el Rugby futbol.* Acharro brought these games. In the old days, Chirican men were warriors. Since Acharro wished us peaceful, he believed these games would better occupy our men. He was correct. Our men have come to like them better than warlike exercises."

"Too much so," put in a sturdy-framed woman whose name, she told us, was Ita. "They do little else. They are all either Caymans or Jaguars, and when they are not playing they sit talking about matches won or lost. They are a little foolish. They are, after all, men.

"We do the handicrafts," Ita continued. "We also raise our children, plant and reap, bake the cassava bread, catch the fish, prepare the meals, feed the chickens. Our mighty warriors," she added wryly, "would do well to learn something useful, too."

"There will soon be no more games or anything else," said Suncha. "Acharro has told us what we face. The Chiricas, all of us, are doomed."

"And you'll calmly accept that?" retorted Vesper. "Is that what you want?"

"No," answered Suncha. "None of us wishes it. We have talked among ourselves, but we can think of no way to turn aside our fate."

"I'm sure you've talked among yourselves," said Vesper. "But you haven't talked about it with me. I want to think it over. Will all of you come here again? Tomorrow?"

"Yes, if you like," replied Suncha, "though I do not know what help you can give us. Indeed, perhaps now it is best for all of us to join our ancestors."

"Your ancestors can get along without you for a while," Vesper said. "A long while, if I have anything to do with it."

That night, after Suncha set up our hammocks, Vesper stayed awake and thoughtful, sitting on a mat in the spill of light from an old oil lamp, an item no doubt provided by Blazer when his trade consisted more of small comforts than arms and ammunition.

"Brinnie?" Vesper shook my hammock. I sat up immediately at the urgent tone in her voice. "Someone's at the window."

It was, I supposed, a curiosity-seeker, perhaps one of the women or some village youngster. Nevertheless, fully alert, I swung to the ground.

A shadow loomed outside. It was quite large. I cast about for some object of defense. Next moment, a figure was in the room.

CHAPTER

12

Lacking a better weapon, I seized the oil lamp. Vesper took a step toward the intruder. It was Acharro.

"Nice of you to visit," Vesper said. "Is it your custom for a chief to climb through windows in the middle of the night?"

"I did not wish to be observed by the watchman at your door." Acharro's face no longer bore streaks of paint. While his bearing was that of a chieftain, his expression held a trace of discomfort. In a lesser personage, I would have called it sheepish. "I hoped we could speak privately."

"That depends on what you want to speak about."

"I have been thinking of our meeting. I must say this to you: If your plan has value, I wish to learn what it is."

"I'm sure you're a splendid chief," said Vesper. "You'd have made a better diplomat. You'd like to have our own private meeting here? It very neatly gets around my speaking to the rest of the council."

"That is not my purpose. When custom is useful, I use it. When it works against us, it must give way. I wished only

to tell you: I agree to let you speak to my council yourself
Tomorrow night we shall hear whatever you offer and
judge for ourselves if you can help."

"Fair enough," said Vesper. "I don't ask more than that
Well, yes, one thing. I want to have a look at Ocotalpa."

"A journey of several days?" Acharro said. "We no
longer go there as we once did. The trails are overgrown
It would be difficult for you."

"More difficult if I don't. I have to, Acharro. Will some
one take us there after the meeting?"

Acharro thought for a while. "If we accept your plan
If it is necessary. Yes. I will lead you there myself."

"I was thinking of something else, too," Vesper added
"When they asked you what the Chiricas could bring to the
national treasury, you forgot something.

"I've seen all the things your women make. They're
marvelous—and valuable. Do you realize that? Blaze
could build up a trade in them. The government would
have money from export licenses—not a fortune, not the El
Dorado the conquistadores searched for, but a nice profit."

"Shall I quote your economist Adam Smith?" Acharro
smiled bleakly. "Or the simple law of supply and demand
We could not produce enough to make the smallest differ
ence. This has always been true of El Dorado. Even Corinto
del Norte in its golden days did not succeed."

"Corinto del Norte? What's that?"

"What it is," replied Acharro, "is nothing. What it was
A city near the headwaters of the Culebra. It was rich in it
time. There were rubber and coffee plantations, much valu
able timber. It prospered more than Puerto Palmas and wa
more beautiful. In Corinto del Norte, they had even buil
an opera house as grand as any in the world."

Acharro, of course, was exaggerating. I doubted that it could match our Academy of Music, but I let his remark go by. Vesper listened with keen interest.

"The plantations dwindled, the timberlands became exhausted," Acharro went on. "Corinto del Norte was abandoned. The city is a ruin. No one lives there, not even the ghosts of its former inhabitants. It is less than a memory."

"I'd like to see it," Vesper said. "Not now," she added, as Acharro raised a hand in protest. "We have a lot to do first. We'll talk about that another time. Right now, I still have something to think about. So, if that's all that's on your mind—"

"One thing more." Acharro looked deeply at Vesper. "It is also our custom for a chief to be wise. I was not. I spoke too quickly when we met. Perhaps I spoke too harshly."

"Right on both counts," said Vesper. "Are you trying to tell me you want to apologize?"

"No," Acharro said. "One does not apologize unless there is the possibility of acceptance."

"Oh?" Vesper grinned at him. "If I tried, I think I could manage an acceptance."

Next morning, I saw little of Acharro. He had said nothing more and had vanished as quickly as he had come. I caught only glimpses of him while he supervised the storage of Blazer's weapons. I did, however, see a great deal of the Chirican women. As promised, they arrived at the schoolhouse where Vesper awaited them. Feeling out of place in such a gathering, I prepared to go wandering around the village.

"Stay here with us," Vesper insisted. "Suncha and Ita

took something of a shine to you. Besides, you might have a thought or two that could help."

I doubted that. I doubted that even Vesper could suggest anything useful. The women themselves had already examined most of the possibilities.

"When the time comes for the men to fight," said Suncha, "Acharro has ordered us to take the youngest children and go into the backlands."

"We do not want to obey that order," said Ita. "We will not let ourselves be scattered through the jungle or see our children turned into beggars in the streets of Puerto Palmas."

"Good for you," said Vesper. "I don't want to see that happen either."

"We have thought of getting hold of some of the rifles," said Suncha, "and teaching ourselves to use them. That way, at least, we can fight beside our men."

"Die with them, too," returned Vesper. "Have you spoken to your men about that?"

"You must know that women do not speak in council meetings," Suncha said.

"I'm going to," said Vesper. "I may be the first; I'll make sure I'm not the last. If you're willing to die in public, you should have the right to talk in public. But I mean, haven't you said anything to your husbands? Your sweethearts?"

"Of course we have," said Ita. "They do not listen. They tell us they will see to all that must be done."

"So far," said Vesper, "all they've seen to is getting killed. If that's their best answer, they should stick to cricket and *el Rugby futbol.*

"I'm thinking out a plan," Vesper went on. "Something

all the village can help with. That's only the beginning. Once this canal business is settled, there's a lot more that needs straightening out. But, first things first. We'll get to them later."

I wanted to take Vesper aside and warn her against making promises she could not keep. I did not have the opportunity. The talk turned from the approaching battle to everyday doings in the village. The women were delighted for the chance to speak up about their work, about the Caymans and Jaguars who mostly issued orders and then went off to play cricket.

Suncha, Ita, and the rest were, as it came out, quite indignant about their situation. Instead of calming them, Vesper stirred them up all the more.

"Fair's fair," Vesper declared. "What it comes down to is plain common sense. Your lives are as valuable as your men's, I'd say. Why shouldn't you have the same rights they do?"

To this, the women heartily and loudly agreed. The talk went on in this vein for the rest of the morning. By the time they left the schoolhouse, I had begun feeling a little apprehensive. I remarked to Vesper that if the Caymans and Jaguars survived they would have more than a canal to deal with. They would have a village full of very determined women.

"I hope so," said Vesper.

The council meeting began at sundown. Vesper and I hurried to the plaza. The Chirican warriors had already assembled in Acharro's *residencia.* At the far end of the room, I saw Blazer with Adelita on his shoulder, Smiler and Slider cross-legged beside him. Flanked by some of the older warriors, Acharro had just entered. He and his village elders bore ceremonial markings on their faces and bodies. Their expressions were as hard-bitten and grim as a Philadelphia charities commission.

Vesper is not a girl to go unnoticed. Instead of making her way unobtrusively, she strode through the crowd of warriors. The Caymans and Jaguars had evidently not been forewarned. At sight of a female in their midst, some of them stared aghast; others protested furiously and shouted at her to begone immediately. Vesper merely smiled at them and proceeded calmly to Acharro's side.

While the position of chieftain may have its satisfactions, I did not envy the poor fellow in that moment. He was, as Vesper might have put it, between a rock and a hard place. On the one hand, he had an extremely agitated body of Caymans and Jaguars. On the other, he had Vesper.

To his credit, he managed remarkably well. His voice rang out above the commotion, and by sheer force of his presence he restored a measure of quiet.

"I have gone against our custom," he declared, "for the sake of something more important: the life of all the Chirican tribe."

Vesper now claimed her turn to address the council. She told them briefly who she was and why we had come, and that she believed she could settle matters without bloodshed.

"First," said Vesper, "as soon as I can, I'll go to Puerto Palmas and send a telegram to my *abogados, los caballeros* Kenge and Carboy. They'll see to it that de Rochefort can never get a legal right to dig up my land. Still, de Rochefort may have some tricks up his sleeve I don't even know about.

"So, meanwhile, we have to delay his work and slow him down as much as we can. This will give me time to set my own plan in motion—something that will make him give up the canal altogether.

"To start, some of you will tear up sections of the railroad track. Some others can make sure the bucket dredge gets a bad case of indigestion. A few of you must get into the camp and join the work crew. I'd guess that a lot of de Rochefort's laborers are still superstitious. You'll quietly spread the idea among them that the old gods are angry, they're against the canal—"

At this, one of the elders broke in, standing up and angrily addressing Vesper.

"Is this what you offer us? Delay? It will not succeed for long, if at all. How do you know, in the end, your lawyers will not prove powerless? You have told us of nothing strong enough to stop the canal here and now, once and for all."

"I was about to mention," said Vesper, "what will send de Rochefort packing. Ocotalpa. It's going to erupt."

My jaw must have dropped. I was thunderstruck by her declaration. I expected a wave of equal astonishment from the council.

There was only silence.

CHAPTER 13

It should have been a glorious moment. Vesper, in her own modest way, was rather pleased with herself and, in my opinion, rightly so. She had confronted an assemblage of Caymans and Jaguars, faced a stern council of elders, and offered to work a miracle that would save all their lives. As she calmly stood there, face shining and eyes bright, I could not have admired her more. I applauded vigorously. I was the only one.

It was a disaster.

After a moment to recover from their shock, the Chiricas exchanged glances of dismay. Acharro looked crushed. He said nothing. The same elder who had spoken before expressed what, alas, was the general opinion.

"We have let you enter our council against our will. We have listened to you, nevertheless. You offered us little to begin with. At the end, you have made fools of us. Did you think to amuse us, like a woman promising to bring her child the moon for a play toy?"

There was no need for a motion of adjournment. The meeting was over, by silent acclamation. The men got to their feet as if suddenly remembering they had something better to do. The twins' round faces were identically glum. Blazer rubbed his nose and stared at the ground. Even Adelita was silent.

"Wait a minute, all of you—" Vesper called to them, although the poor child realized it was too late. She did not burst into tears, I would not have blamed her if she had. On the contrary, her eyes flashed and her jaw was set.

Acharro's elders, meantime, had vacated the *residencia.* Blazer and the twins offered a few words of consolation before they drifted out. As for Acharro, he was taking the business very personally. He looked at Vesper more in sorrow than anger, and with a sort of anguished disbelief. The poor fellow had evidently set more store in her plan than he had been willing to admit. He had, of course, every reason to be disappointed, but he seemed more crestfallen than I would have expected for a chieftain.

"Next time," declared Vesper, "they'll listen."

"There will not be a next time," Acharro said bitterly.

"Of course there will. As soon as we get back from Ocotalpa. This doesn't change anything," she went on, as Acharro frowned at her. "I'm still going there."

"To do what?" Acharro demanded. "There is no purpose in it."

"If I told you now," said Vesper, "you'd only start arguing with me. Put it this way: I want to go, and you promised you'd take us. Is it your custom to break your word?"

"I said I would do so if I accepted your plan."

"You haven't heard my plan," said Vesper, "so you don't know if you'll accept it or not."

If there was some flaw in this line of reasoning, Acharro seemed unable to put his finger on it. Finally, as Vesper continued to press him, he agreed.

Ordinarily, I would not have allowed Vesper to go traipsing off into a jungle to face anacondas, *tigres,* giant spiders, and whatever else. In this case, given the general attitude of the Caymans and Jaguars toward her, the jungle seemed a better place than the village.

Acharro, with half a dozen of his Chiricas carrying rifles and provisions, came to escort us early next morning. We set out from the village, heading more or less north. Acharro had spoken accurately. The trails were overgrown and invisible—to us, at any rate—though Acharro knew precisely where he was going, as if he sensed the old pathways under his feet.

Leading us, he seemed to put aside any ill feelings he might have had. It would have been difficult to do otherwise, for this area had a quality different from the steamy tangle of the riverbank. The trees rose to meet high above us in cathedral-like arches and canopies. Pale green light filtered through the leaves and, from time to time, rays of sunlight fell in great golden shafts. A strange tranquility muted even the chatterings of birds and monkeys.

"Blazer told us your ancestors are buried here," Vesper said quietly, when we halted.

"Here and everywhere. You will not see their graves," Acharro added, when Vesper questioned him about this. "It is not our custom to raise mounds or monuments." He gestured around him. "This is monument enough. They have returned to the earth, and the earth has welcomed them home.

"We have not made our land sacred. Our ancestors have done so. To destroy any part of it would be to destroy their living presence.

"I am not speaking of ghosts. We no longer believe in such. That is crude superstition. Yet, our ancestors live within the earth, trees, vines, and flowers, in the cries of each wild creature and the songs of birds. This is not an empty shell like Corinto del Norte. That city is dead because it was never truly alive."

Vesper put a hand on his arm. Before she could speak, Acharro continued, "I will give you one chance, no more. Otherwise, we shall attack the work camp as my father and I have decided. We have canoes ready in the inlets and are building more. Some of us shall use them to go downriver. The *Libertador* will carry still others. We will strike from the shore, all along the banks. That is our plan. You will have to show me that yours is better."

To me, his plan would succeed in one thing: getting them all killed. Which, of course, was what they wanted. I said nothing. My opinion had not been solicited. Vesper, surely, saw it as plainly as I did. For once, she did not offer any criticism.

"Right now," she said, "let's just get a move on."

All that day, as we pressed ahead, the ground had been continually rising, so gently, at first, that I was hardly aware of it. By the time we camped again, the going had grown so steep that I was glad to rest. Vesper would have pushed on a few hours more, but this Acharro refused to do.

The landscape was changing noticeably. We crossed a

number of open, scrabbly stretches before plunging again into jungle. From one such clearing, we caught our first good sight of Ocotalpa, its green cone rising ahead of us, jutting above the forest canopy surrounding it.

"It's bigger than it looked on the map." Vesper put her hands on her hips and observed the brooding height with satisfaction. "It should do nicely."

Acharro and his men eyed the ragged peak, broken like the top of a ruined tower, with a certain reverence. So did Vesper.

"What it must have been like," she said in a hushed voice. "The flames, the boiling lava— I'm sorry I missed all that."

"Do not be sorry," said Acharro. "In ancient times, the *indios* made human sacrifices to it. You would not have wished to be there. Nor would I." He gave Vesper half a smile. "It is no longer our custom."

"I didn't think it would be," said Vesper.

Having looked her fill at Ocotalpa, Acharro and I expected her to start back to the village.

"I haven't come this far just to gawk," Vesper said. "I want to really see it, look inside. I have to find out what's there."

Acharro assured her there was only the overgrown crater and some outcroppings of old lava. Vesper insisted. Finally, Acharro sighed and shrugged.

"If you have brought me on a fool's errand," he tartly said, "I might as well be all the way a fool."

I assumed he would head straight for the summit. Instead, he bore to his left, where the ground had flattened somewhat. This, he explained, was the old sacrificial trail.

It was not too badly obstructed, all things considered, and he set a good pace.

The trail, however, was not a fragrant one. After a time, Vesper wrinkled her nose and sniffed the air. At the beginning of a large, lopsided clearing, she strode quickly ahead.

"I remember this lake from my map," she called back. "Here it is, Brinnie. But—it isn't water."

CHAPTER

14

Vesper halted to look across a wide expanse of what appeared neither liquid nor solid, yet both at the same time. Toward its center, black bubbles rose continually to the surface, where some burst and others congealed into humps and ridges. Shreds of vapor hung in the air. The aroma was tantalizingly familiar.

"Tar," Vesper called. "A lake of it."

I could only stare in appreciation of this phenomenon of nature. I knew of Venezuela's renowned Lake Guanoco and its thousand acres of asphaltum. This, in comparison, was small but nevertheless remarkable, seething and simmering with a life of its own.

The edges had hardened into a thick skin. Before I knew it, Vesper had stepped out and taken a few paces toward the bubbling center. She bent and ran a hand across the surface.

Acharro streaked past me. I had never seen a man move so fast. In one motion, he seized her under the arms, snatched her up, and whirled around to spring onto firmer ground.

"Matasombra would have eaten you alive," he burst out, more relieved than angry. "There are ways to cross it safely. Until you know them, stay clear of this place."

"Thank you, Acharro," said Vesper, "but I was perfectly all right."

"You would not have been the first to think so. You could have found yourself at the bottom along with unwary animals, and some unwary conquistadores, too. They called it 'Palangana del Diablo,' the Devil's Washbasin, and no doubt had good reason to name it so."

Vesper examined the palms of her hands besmirched with a dark film. "Do you realize what this is?"

"The sweat of the gods? The blood of Matasombra?" Acharro gave her an amused look. "Otherwise, a compound of hydrogen and carbon. You do not need to instruct me in organic chemistry."

"Do you also realize there must be oil deposits all around here?"

"And now you will teach me geology? I am quite aware of that."

"You told me the Chiricas had nothing of value. Do you really understand—?"

"Thoroughly," Acharro retorted. "Do you think I would follow the example of Drake in your own Pennsylvania? That I would allow speculators to bore, drill, strip away this land to make room for machinery? That would destroy us as much as the canal—in a different fashion, but just as surely."

"I hate to keep reminding you, but it's my land," said Vesper. "Don't worry. I wouldn't allow it either. De Rochefort must know it's here," she added. "He had geologists survey Ocotalpa. They'd have told him."

"What he does or does not know is of little interest," said Acharro. "Will he next turn his attention to Matasombra? He will not have the opportunity. He may take my life, but I promise you I will take his."

Acharro refused further discussion. He insisted we begin our ascent so that we could start back to the village and be well on our way before nightfall. We followed while he and his Chiricas skirted the lake of tar and struck upward along traces of an ancient pathway. In its day, it had been hard packed and no doubt continually repaired. Overgrown though it was, our ascent proved quicker and easier than I expected.

Along the trail, Vesper caught sight of a number of carved wooden figures, perhaps representing the guards or priests of Ocotalpa. Fallen, eroded, tangled in creepers and yellow-flowered thornbushes, their moldering features stared impassively. Vesper would have stopped to examine them, but Acharro's patience was running out and she wisely decided not to test it.

When we reached the crater, we found it exactly as Acharro had told us. The rich soil had spawned abundant vegetation around the rim. The inner wall of the crater itself sloped at a gentle angle to a lava dome at the bottom. I had the impression that a faint reek of sulfur still hung in the air.

Vesper, to my relief, did not propose climbing down Ocotalpa's gullet. She clambered around the rim, observing its configuration, scuffing her feet against the outcroppings.

"Nice." Vesper nodded as if Ocotalpa had been awaiting her approval. "I had to see if there were chimneys or flues, or any sort of crevices. There aren't, but it doesn't matter. It will be a fine eruption. I hadn't known about Matasombra. That should make it perfect."

"I have brought you here, I have shown you what you asked." Acharro made a commendable effort to speak quietly and patiently. "Do you still say you will bring a dead volcano to life?"

"Of course not. Nobody can."

"A fool's errand," Acharro muttered. "As I knew it would be."

"It won't erupt," said Vesper. "De Rochefort's going to think it will. That's what counts.

"I started thinking about it when Brinnie and I were in the jungle. The chameleons change color to match wherever they are; on a leaf, they're green, on a piece of wood, brown. Some of the insects—you can't tell them from twigs or mushrooms. It's only a disguise, but good enough to fool their enemies. No, Ocotalpa won't erupt. It'll look as if it's going to.

"First, I thought we could use gunpowder. You have plenty of that. But we don't need to. Put your people to work, women, children, Caymans, Jaguars, the lot, and we'll do it in no time. Make the biggest torches, as many as you can. Soak them in tar from the lake. Chop out big lumps of it. Line the crater with them, fill it up, then—"

"Set them on fire?" broke in Acharro. "Is that what you intend?"

"Exactly." Vesper beamed at him. "You'll have the biggest, blackest cloud of smoke anyone's ever seen. Ocotalpa's going to look ready to blow at any moment.

"You might like to pack in some gunpowder anyway," she added. "Just for a little frosting on the cake."

Acharro said nothing for a time. He peered down into the crater, then looked out over the forest. He made an abrupt motion with his head. "Come. We must return to the village."

"You're being impossible," Vesper burst out. "There's nothing wrong with my idea. You'd call it wonderful if you'd thought of it yourself—or one of your Caymans or Jaguars came up with it. What's the harm of trying? You won't be worse off than you are. It can work. I know it can."

"So do I," said Acharro. "It is excellent. Why did you assume I refused it? We shall do it, and everything else that you suggested."

Vesper was as close to being at a loss for words as I had ever seen her. The dear girl was almost taken aback, but only for an instant.

"Now you're being sensible," she said. "I don't see how we can fail. When de Rochefort sees smoke pouring out of Ocotalpa's mouth, he's logically going to put two and two together. In this case, he'll come up with the wrong answer. The wrong one for him, the right one for us.

"I knew it was a good plan, but what finally convinced me—well, Acharro, it was you. Do you remember what you said the first time we met? About making assumptions? Forming your opinion in advance from what you've known before and what you think is logical? It applies to de Rochefort, too."

"I was angry when I said that," replied Acharro. "At the time, I assumed you were less than what you were."

"Well," said Vesper, "you turned out to be more than I assumed you were. So we're even."

Acharro was impatient to return and set Vesper's plan in train. To lose not a moment, as we left Ocotalpa and skirted Matasombra, he ordered three of his Chiricas to stay there and begin preparations immediately, gathering whatever was suitable to burn, making as much as possible ready for the villagers.

Though he pushed us and the remainder of his men to the limit, at nightfall he allowed us to halt. We had, however, made excellent progress. We would start again early next morning and soon be in the village.

We never reached it.

CHAPTER

15

They attacked us at daybreak; I could not guess how many, for they burst upon us so suddenly. I was seized even before I could spring to my feet, their approach had been too stealthy to rouse me. The Chirican night guard and Acharro himself must have been sharp-eared enough to detect suspicious noises no matter how faint—I had the confused impression they were already up, weapons in hand. There were some shots, and flashes from the rifle muzzles. I had no inclination to wonder who was firing at whom, or why. My thoughts were only for Vesper, shouting furiously at the top of her voice. Though I saw little more than black shadows milling in the faint greenish haze, I tried with all strength to shake free and reach her.

"Brinnie? Where are you?"

I lunged in the direction of her cry above the racket of gunfire, while the alarmed jungle creatures shrieked and jabbered. In a last effort, I tore myself loose from one of my assailants. Another grappled me and clung doggedly as I heaved my way toward the dear girl.

Acharro was fighting to do likewise. Tallest of the struggling figures, he was swinging his rifle like a club and calling Vesper's name. His opponents held him at bay; he could not help us, nor could we help him. I deeply regretted the absence of my revolver.

They worked quickly, wordlessly except for a few gruff instructions to one another. By the time I reached Vesper, they had tied her hands and now applied similar treatment to me. Though I forcefully ordered them to release us, they paid no heed. Having bound us securely, they sent us both stumbling on ahead of them.

"Acharro!" Vesper cried. "Here—"

Her voice went suddenly muffled. One of the ruffians had thrust Vesper's bandana into her mouth. Another forced some vile rag into my own—I dreaded to think it might be his handkerchief. Clearly, these were men without scruples or sense of human decency.

I vainly hoped that the sounds of the fray would somehow reach Acharro's men at the lake, though knowing full well they were long out of earshot. They would, in any case, have come too late. We were shoved, dragged, hurried along despite Vesper's attempts to dig in her heels and do all possible to hinder our abductors. Our captors, I was now able to see, numbered five not counting those who remained behind to engage Acharro and his Chiricas. They were a villainous looking crew.

Only after we had gone some good distance and these wretches were satisfied they were not pursued by the Chiricas did they show sufficient glimmerings of mercy to remove our gags. Vesper immediately voiced the indignation and outrage that the bandana, until now, had muted. Our captors not only refused to answer her barrage of angry questions, they threatened to stifle us both again if she kept on. They allowed us, though grudgingly, a few sips of water from their evil smelling canteens.

"One good thing," Vesper muttered as they prodded us along. "They're not going to kill us. Yet. If they were, they'd have done it back there." She glanced over her shoulder. "Acharro— Brinnie, what happened to him and the other Chiricas? They could all have been killed, badly hurt—"

The unknown fate of Acharro and his people distressed her more than our own plight, which was far from enviable. Our abductors rarely halted, forcing us to keep up a grueling pace that brought us ever farther from hope of rescue. Even so, Vesper refused to despair.

"They'll come looking for us. They know the jungle better than this pack of baboons. They're de Rochefort's, I'm sure of it. I recognize one of them from the work camp.

"When he didn't find us downriver," she went on, "he naturally started searching upriver. Now they've got us, though, why aren't they taking us to the camp or Puerto Palmas? We're not going that way at all."

Vesper's unerring sense of direction had accurately discerned our path as heading nearly due west. She pondered this a while, but at last gave up seeking an answer.

"I don't know what they have in mind," she said. "Wherever they take us, the Chiricas can follow our trail."

The dear girl's confidence raised my own spirits for the rest of the day. Close to nightfall, however, my hopes shattered, and perhaps even Vesper's were a little rickety. The Chiricas, by skill and experience, could unquestionably pick up the faintest of trails in the jungle. Could they do as much over water?

"The Culebra," Vesper murmured. "There, straight on." Her voice faltered slightly. "Brinnie—they have a boat."

At the riverbank, Vesper's eyes fixed on a vessel standing out in midstream. Though shadows fell rapidly, it was still possible to make out the shape of a large craft. One of our abductors lit a makeshift torch of dead branches. An answering light flared from the boat. Moments later, a dinghy cast loose from the vessel's stern and made rapidly for shore.

Our captors obliged us to clamber aboard. The oarsmen immediately struck for the waiting craft, which loomed all the larger as we neared it.

"A yacht?" Vesper squinted at the long, sleek outline. "De Rochefort does nicely for himself."

In better circumstances I would have admired it more. It was indeed a trim, handsome vessel, no doubt very swift in the water, its lines unbroken by paddle wheels. No sails, however, had been unfurled from the masts.

"Interesting," said Vesper. "It must have one of those fancy screw propellers. Oceangoing, too, I'd guess. Nothing but the best."

Nautical engineering design was a subject furthest from my mind as the dinghy pulled up alongside. Our hands were unbound so that we could scramble up a rope ladder to the deck. Still rubbing our aching arms and wrists, we were prodded down a short companionway and, without a word of explanation, shoved into a cabin.

"Very snug—for a prison cell." Vesper began investigating our quarters as soon as the door was slammed shut and bolted after us. Without a lamp, it was difficult to make out the appointments in detail. I groped my way to a double berth set into the bulkhead.

Vesper called me to help her open the porthole. Between the two of us, we could not budge it.

"Sealed," she muttered. "Like the train window." She dropped to hands and knees, searching around the carpeted deck. "I thought there might be another *escupidera.* It helped before."

Such a receptacle, even if available, would not have benefited us.

"We could still smash the glass." Vesper returned to the porthole. "Kick it out— No, that won't do any good. I can't squeeze through. Even if I could—Brinnie, there's no way at all you'd manage.

"We're moving," she added. "Well, it beats walking to Puerto Palmas. Wait—that's odd. We're not going there. We're heading upriver."

Vesper had given up any further attempt at escape from our cell, as I must call our stateroom. Resigned to awaiting whatever lay in store, and to deal with new circumstances as they presented themselves, she climbed into the upper berth. But her thoughts returned to Acharro.

"He can't be dead. I won't believe that, Brinnie. Not Acharro."

I agreed with her, more out of consolation than conviction. The dear girl could not bear the idea of that splendid young chieftain sprawled lifeless in the jungle, nor could I. Alas, he would not have been the first. The conquistadores had taken their heavy toll centuries before. De Rochefort's gang would not hesitate now to do the same. I did not say this to Vesper; privately, I feared the worst.

Despite her uncanny ability to sleep, if she chooses, in the midst of any disaster, the dear girl tossed as restlessly as I did.

The ship's bells chiming midnight brought me out of a fitful doze. Much scuffling of feet sounded above deck, and voices called out orders. Vesper, at the porthole, looked out over the moonswept river.

"We're putting in. We're here—wherever that may be."

The yacht lurched a little, the noise of the engines changed in pitch. Our door flung open. Once again, our captors laid hands on us and sent us clambering up the companionway.

Torches had been set about the landing stage. In the flickering light, I could not be certain that the men who took us in charge at the end of the gangplank were our original captors or yet another band of ruffians. Their behavior was equally crude. They fell in around us and at rifle point forced us to trot from what must, at one time, have been extensive port facilities. The warehouses now stood roofless, most of the walls had crumbled; it was barely more than the skeleton of a harbor.

"Corinto del Norte," Vesper murmured to me as we were jostled along an *avenida* of broken paving stones. "Must be. Acharro said it was abandoned. What's this gang of thugs doing here?"

We crossed the ruined plaza. The moon was enormous above the mountains just beyond the city. The pale brilliance flooded over the deserted buildings, fallen tiles, and empty eye sockets of windows. The air was almost chilly.

We were escorted through a sagging iron gate into an overgrown courtyard. It was large, modeled after a Spanish cloister. I judged it had been the residence of some long-departed grandee, perhaps the *alcalde* himself. We passed through a vacant salon furnished mainly with spiderwebs and shadows.

A sudden burst of illumination dazzled me. I heard Vesper's sharp intake of breath. From the ceiling of this spacious room hung a crystal chandelier ablaze with light. Massive candelabra stood on the long table, four place settings of ornate silver service gleamed on the spotless cloth.

At the far end sat a figure in an immaculate white dinner jacket. He rose and gestured for our captors to stand away.

"Mademoiselle Holly. Professor."

De Rochefort bowed curtly. The villain at least did not have the temerity to kiss Vesper's hand. He gave her, instead, an apologetic, almost wistful smile.

"I fear you have not had the most pleasant of journeys. I hope your cabin aboard the *Midas* was not too uncomfortable."

Vesper's response did not imitate the formality of de Rochefort's greeting.

"You," she remarked, "you despicable, miserable—pelican!"

"The pelican, like the poet, acts from necessity," de Rochefort said. "You have every reason to feel outraged. I implore you, nevertheless, not to think of me too severely."

"I don't want to think of you at all," retorted Vesper.

"Tell me straight out what you're up to. Then put Brinnie and me on your yacht and sail us to Acharro's village. If you've done him or his people any harm—"

"I would like nothing better than to grant your request," said de Rochefort. "I regret—profoundly, believe me—that is not possible."

"Then make it possible—" Vesper's voice broke off. Her eyes had gone to the doorway.

I followed her gaze. The new arrival was resplendent in full dinner dress. At sight of his shock of white hair, his large looming form, the cheerful smile spreading over his suntanned features, my heart sank.

In that dreadful moment of recognition, I knew our doom was sealed.

"Good evening," said Dr. Helvitius, with great cordiality. "What a pleasure to see you again."

CHAPTER

16

"The pleasure," said Vesper, "is all yours."

The dear girl faced him squarely. If she felt the same despair I did, she denied him the satisfaction of seeing it. Her glance did not waver. Her features held the expression of calm courage she displayed at our last encounter with the abominable creature. On that unhappy occasion, Helvitius had bent every effort to destroy us by means of dynamite bombs. His failure had no doubt continued to rankle. As Vesper observed at the time, he was not the sort to forgive and forget.

Dr. Desmond Helvitius has been, for me, a source of deep personal disappointment. A man of scholarly achievement, in addition to incalculable wealth, of high academic qualifications in science and technology, in classical antiquities, a contributor to journals of chemistry, physics, biology —it distresses me to consider that an individual of such capabilities should also be the most reprehensible of arch-villains. Worse, this did not appear to trouble him. I had o conclude he was deficient in any sense of moral duty or elf-respect. A harsh judgment to make on a colleague, and do so reluctantly. The fellow is a disgrace to the academic profession.

Following Vesper's example, I tried to put a brazen face on a bad situation. Whatever might be my inner agitation, he could not fail to detect the tone of scorn in my voice.

"You, sir, appear to have found a new employment: serving a scoundrel as treacherous as yourself."

"Brinnie, somehow I don't think that's the way it is," Vesper said to me.

"Miss Holly is correct," said Helvitius. "Monsieur de Rochefort serves me—and serves me well. There is no question who is master. *N'est-ce pas,* Alain?"

De Rochefort said nothing. His features tightened as Dr. Helvitius continued.

"It was I who instructed him to send the telegram I hoped you would find irresistible, as, in fact, you did. If you had not, I would have resorted to other means. In all his actions, he merely obeyed my orders. He had little choice."

Helvitius smiled benevolently at de Rochefort. "An unfortunate young man. Having no inclination to shoot himself, he would like nothing better than to shoot me. He will not. He understands that if he attempted anything so foolish, at my demise certain documents would automatically be made public.

"I refer to evidence of his crime. Alain is a brilliant engineer. In other areas, he is less intelligent. He suffers from certain flaws of character. For one, gambling.

"Alas, how Dame Fortune toys with us. In Alain's case, she brought him to ruin. His gambling debts only doubled and trebled the more he sought to mend his losses. At risk were his ancestral château, his personal fortune, all his possessions to the very clothes on his back.

"Another flaw is his peculiar sense of honor. Faced with such a burden, a sensible person would contrive to—shall we say—liquidate his debtors rather than his debts. Gambling debts, however, are gentlemen's obligations. He chose to pay them.

"Thinking it better to be a thief than a defaulter, he embezzled a very large sum from the finances of the recent Suez Canal venture in which he played a distinguished role. As I myself did," Helvitius added, "naturally under a different identity. It was I who discovered his peculations.

"I could have sent him to prison then and there. I chose otherwise. A man of his talents would be useful to me in other enterprises, El Dorado, for one. Not only the canal, but the Matasombra oil deposits. Out of my own pocket, I replaced the embezzled money and protected him against discovery. I counted it a wise investment. So it has proved. Alain is efficient in his tasks—except in the matter of your escape. He has made up for that by finding you and bringing you here."

De Rochefort's face, during this, had drained its color. Even his lips had gone pale with rage and shame. I have never seen a man exposed to such humiliation. He stood up, turned on his heel, and was about to stride from the room.

"Remain," commanded Helvitius. "Our guests will be interested in some of the technical details of my project. You are in the best position to provide them."

De Rochefort hesitated, then silently took his place again.

"You're wrong," Vesper said to Helvitius. "I don't care a rap for your technical details. Whatever you're doing, you can tell me pretty quickly. After that, I warn you—"

"Dear girl," I cried, "his vile purpose is all too clear. You thwarted him once. His diabolical arrogance cannot stomach that. Revenge—"

"Revenge is a crude word," Helvitius interrupted. "Call it a simple balancing of accounts. It is the least of my motives. Whether or not Miss Holly is interested, I urge you both to seat yourselves. I promise you an excellent supper. Enjoy it, sir. You may not have another such occasion."

This, to me, was the final straw. "How dare you, sir! Invite us to join you at your table? To break bread with you? Sir, you have no sense of propriety."

"Brinnie," said Vesper, "sit down and eat."

First astonished, I realized the dear girl was wiser than I. Though dining with a man who surely intended to kill us went against her every moral fiber, principle must sometimes give way to practicality. Vesper had understood that we must build up our strength to face whatever awaited us. Also, she was very hungry.

"It will not be poisoned," said Helvitius. "I give you my word."

He snapped his fingers and a couple of the guards withdrew, soon returning with silver platters and serving dishes. I was relieved to see Helvitius take portions of the same food we ate. It was, I admit, excellent.

"Who's your cook?" asked Vesper between mouthfuls.

"I am," replied Helvitius. "The art of the cuisine is one of my keen personal pleasures. I would hardly trust my digestion to the mercies of these"—he waved toward the guards—"these barbarians."

Supper with Dr. Helvitius, for all its elegance, was one of the most bizarre and grotesque of my culinary experiences. Contrasted with the attire of Helvitius and de Rochefort, Vesper and I made a pair of wretched scarecrows in our torn, bespattered garments. Our waiters went about their business with rifles and cartridge belts over their shoulders. Silent, de Rochefort barely picked at his food. Helvitius attacked his and did not stint. With each course, he grew more expansive in body and mood. Finally, he dabbed his lips with his napkin and leaned back in his chair.

"A pity that you have seen so little of Corinto," he began. "You would appreciate all the more what I plan for it. I intend to rebuild the mansions, the promenades, the opera house. Most certainly, the opera house. I shall employ the most glorious voice of our time, the divine prima donna Madam Adelina Patti, of whom I am a devoted admirer. She visited Corinto a few years past, on her tour of the West Indies, and was charmed by it. She expressed a hope that the opera house would some day be restored. So it shall.

"The opening performance: *Rigoletto,* with *la diva* Patti as Gilda, naturally. Professor Garrett spoke of revenge. Do you know *Rigoletto?*"

"Things didn't go as Rigoletto planned," said Vesper. "Revenge can boomerang. Keep that in mind."

"In this case, your advice does not apply," said Helvitius. "I control all the circumstances, as I shall control the canal. As you may by now have surmised, my wealth and willpower are the driving force. The canal is mine."

"You're forgetting the government of El Dorado," said Vesper. "And me."

Helvitius shrugged. "Wealth purchases what it pleases, a canal or a country. In the course of time, it is I who shall also control El Dorado. Corinto del Norte will be my *residencia.* El Dorado will continue as a republic—in name if not in fact—with myself its lifetime *presidente.*"

"Monstrous!" I burst out. "A madman's dream!"

"Knowing him," said Vesper, "he might just do it."

"Thank you for your confidence." Helvitius inclined his head. "As for you, Miss Holly, you will help me achieve my goal. Not you personally. Your landholdings.

"Your ownership presents a small difficulty. The government of El Dorado requires permission of the official proprietor. A mere formality. I could, of course, buy the land from you, thus making myself the owner of record, or offer to spare your life in exchange. I will not insult your intelligence by doing either. Now that your life is in my hands, you must realize you will not regain it."

"You've insulted my intelligence if you think I'll let you get away with it," replied Vesper. "Mere formality? You're a lot more worried than you let on. You're out on a limb. If you don't get title to my property, there goes your canal."

"Bluntly put," said Helvitius, "but in essence correct."

"I won't sell, I won't sign the land over to you," said Vesper. "Killing us won't help you. One thing you've overlooked. I've written my will and there's a provision: If anything happens to me, all my property goes to Brinnie and Aunt Mary. If anything happens to Brinnie, it still goes to Aunt Mary. Whether I'm dead or alive, there's no way you'll get your hands on it."

"You think not?" Helvitius smiled at her. "One thing that you, Miss Holly, have overlooked: By El Dorado law, on the death of its owner, property can pass only to a direct offspring. Your will has no validity here.

"Professor Garrett and his wife are your guardians, not your descendants. On your demise, your property will become available to the highest bidder. In short, to me."

Vesper did not reply. Though she did not show it, I knew this revelation had taken even her by surprise.

"At the proper moment," said Helvitius, "I shall supply the authorities with proof of your death—by natural causes. The law will be satisfied, the small technical problem eliminated along with you and Professor Garrett." He turned to de Rochefort. "I remind you, Alain, to go ahead with the new operations we discussed, and to do so with all promptness. I no longer require you here. You are excused."

"Don't let him tangle you in this," Vesper called to de Rochefort as he rose obediently. "You're better off facing up to stealing the money. Otherwise, you'll do his dirty work for the rest of your life."

De Rochefort, avoiding her eyes, quickly left the dining room. Helvitius now addressed Vesper.

"You see, Miss Holly, why I suggested that you enjoy your meal. Henceforth, your situation will not be so agreeable."

One of his ruffians, meantime, had carried in a tray of cordials, brandies, and a silver urn of cocoa. I had neither heart nor stomach for these. Yet, uncertain when we might have food again, I forced myself to choose a cup of thick *chocolatl* and urged Vesper to do the same. Helvitius savored a glass of Napoleon brandy. Having pronounced our death sentence, he was in the friendliest of spirits.

"To put your minds at ease," he said, "be sure I would not dream of unduly hastening your—departure. That will, to some extent, depend on yourselves."

Helvitius rambled on with no thread to his conversation. The heavy meal must have gone to his head, for his remarks made no sense to me. I felt exhausted, even the possibility of my forthcoming demise bore no weight of reality. I turned my confused thoughts to Vesper, hoping for a scheme that would keep her from sharing my fate. The poor child looked sleepy, heavy-eyed. Despite my efforts, my chin dropped to my chest.

"*Au revoir,*" said Helvitius.

CHAPTER

17

"You're not poisoned. Neither am I."

Vesper was shaking me. I begged her to stop, out of mercy for the dismal condition of my stomach and an ache that felt larger than my head. I sat up on the sagging wooden floor of some kind of storage room where, I supposed, we had been carried while unconscious. Plaster had fallen in jagged plaques from the walls, the rafters of the ceiling threatened to give way at any moment.

"Helvitius told the truth—more or less," said Vesper. "He didn't poison us. But he didn't say anything about not giving us a sleeping potion."

"Dear girl," I said, "be thankful he didn't give us anything stronger."

"That's what bothers me. He could have got rid of us then and there. For that matter, he could have saved himself the trouble of feeding us dinner."

Perhaps, I suggested, he might still retain some spark of human decency. He was, I reminded her, an opera lover.

"Whatever he has in mind, I'm sure it's good. For him. Not us. The important thing is: What do *we* have in mind?"

Vesper strode to the single window barred by a rusted iron grille. While my limbs were stiff and my senses still fuzzy, the dear child seemed actually to have benefited from the potion and all the better for a night's sound sleep. If a night it was.

"We could have been unconscious," I told her, "for—who knows how long?"

Vesper nodded. "While you were asleep, I tried to work that out. Where this place is—and when. You're right, Brinnie. It could be the middle of next week. How could we be sure? It was close to noon, by the sun, when I woke up. That's been a few hours. But—what day?

"I'm just going to suppose we've only been here overnight. Say that Helvitius probably wanted us unconscious long enough to lock us up. Even so, how long it's been doesn't matter very much. I want to know where we are—and how we get out.

"It's a creepy sort of feeling, though," added Vesper, "as if I didn't have my feet on solid ground. I don't like not knowing if we'll be hauled out of here in another hour, tomorrow, or ten minutes from now."

"Or left to starve?" My own suggestion did not raise my spirits. "I'm starting to remember a little more. That vile monster spoke about death from natural causes. All he needs to do is wait."

"He won't," said Vesper. "Not that long. It doesn't matter. Since we can't be sure what he'll do, at least we can be sure of what we'll do." She glanced toward the door.

"Keep your voice down, Brinnie. There's a guard outside. I've heard him. He hums off-key."

She beckoned me to the window. "We aren't in the middle of Corinto, that's sure. I'd say an old mansion at the edge of town. See—the forest starts just beyond."

I peered out over what had been a courtyard and formal garden, now strangled by creepers. The remains of a stone wall circled it. Vesper went on, "We'll head south, but stay as far as we can from the river. It's the long way, but the highlands aren't as overgrown as the jungle. We'll have a little easier going. Once we sight Ocotalpa, we'll head for Acharro's village."

Much as I admired the dear girl's unquenchable optimism, she was talking as if we were already free. I wondered if the sleeping draught had worked some harm on her mentality.

"It shouldn't be too hard getting past the wall," said Vesper. "Part of it's down. We won't have to climb. We can squeeze through."

As she indicated, the courtyard's far wall had crumbled, leaving a fair-sized gap between the broken stones.

"I haven't seen guards there. We'll have a clear run," said Vesper. "All it comes down to, Brinnie, is getting into the courtyard."

We were, I hurried to point out, on the second floor. Even if we somehow tore out the grille, we would be hardly better off. Jumping from the window, we stood an excellent chance of breaking our legs or ankles, if not our necks.

"We won't jump. They carried us up. So, we'll go out the way we came in. There has to be a stairway."

More than ever I was convinced Vesper suffered some

lingering effect of the potion. I agreed there would be a stairway, but reminded her of the guard outside.

"Yes," Vesper said. "He's outside. We want him inside. Start breaking up that table in the corner."

Vesper's agile mind had, as usual, far outraced my own. I could not grasp what plan she had concocted.

"It's the same idea as Ocotalpa," Vesper explained. "We'll make it seem to erupt. Here, we'll make it seem as if we're getting out. Come on, now make all the racket you can."

While I set about smashing the table, Vesper stamped around the room.

"I don't know if they searched us," she called loudly to me. "What luck, anyway, they didn't find all these blasting caps. Go ahead, Brinnie, barricade the door. We don't dare have the guard in here."

Vesper continued giving orders, making sure the guard heard every word. Had I closed my eyes and listened, she would have convinced me that serious demolition work was in train instead of two wretched captives playing a desperate charade.

"We'll be out in no time," Vesper declared for the sole benefit of the guard who, by now, must have grown alarmed at what he imagined to be taking place.

"*¡Atención!*" cried Vesper. "*¡Muy explosivo!* Stay back in the corner. Cover your head. It'll blow half the place apart, door and all."

At this, the terror-stricken guard burst into the room, rifle at the ready. If he expected some infernal machine about to explode, he had no time to realize the device was his own mental creation.

I sprang upon him. Unwilling though I am to do violence with malice aforethought, I delivered a vigorous blow with the table leg to the ruffian's cranium. I recognized him as the one who had so brutally gagged Vesper with the bandana. This went a long way toward minimizing my reluctance.

"The stairs, Brinnie!"

Vesper darted past me. I snatched up the guard's rifle. I would have taken the bandolier of cartridges he wore over his shoulder, but the unconscious lout had sprawled so awkwardly I could not disentangle it from him. Regretfully, I had to leave it behind.

We went half sliding half stumbling down a flight of rotting, termite-eaten steps and into the ruined courtyard. Vesper headed for the wall. Her calculations had been excellent. There were no other guards; it was only a matter of a few hundred feet before we gained the breach and scrambled without difficulty through the gap in the masonry.

We hoped to be well on our way before the guard regained enough of his wits to raise the alarm. There was a good possibility of doing so, for the highlands around Corinto del Norte presented a landscape different from the lower reaches of the Culebra. Here, alternating with areas of forest, we found gravelly passages and open stretches of grassland. Vesper struck on what must have been an old hunting trail running more or less south.

"Should we follow it?" Vesper glanced at the wide meadow on either side of us. "There's not much cover."

In my view, we had a good head start and should make the most of our advantage. The trail was fairly smooth and would take us quickly out of reach.

"If we found it," said Vesper, "Helvitius must know about it, too."

The abominable scoundrel, I reminded her, would be some distance behind. It would soon be nightfall, when it would be unwise to travel at all. At that point, we could turn off and find a hiding place until morning. We agreed, finally, to hold to the path a short while.

Vesper paced along warily. I had begun to breathe a little easier, all the more since we were no longer unarmed and defenseless. From time to time, I glanced back to make certain we were not pursued.

I would have done better to look ahead. Vesper saw them before I did. A party of horsemen were making their way toward us. The downward sloping ground had concealed them until they were almost upon us.

It was the vile Helvitius and half a dozen of his ruffians.

Vesper instantly struck out across the meadow, seeking the protection of the forest beyond. I could hardly believe my eyes. I halted a bewildered moment, then set after her. The villainous crew kicked their horses into a gallop.

Even Vesper's lithe legs were no match for them. The ruffians spread out on either side, while Helvitius bore down upon us. I faced him and unslung the rifle.

"The girl—quickly!" commanded Helvitius. He sprang from his horse. His hirelings had already surrounded Vesper. Two dismounted, seized and dragged her toward their master.

I raised the rifle. "Order your men to unhand her and stand away."

"After the inconvenience of regaining your pleasant company? Professor Garrett, you can hardly expect me to do so."

"I warn you, sir," I replied. "It is only proper for me to advise you that I will not hesitate to fire."

"Will you not?" Helvitius gave a wry smile. He motioned to one of his crew. "Take him. Tie him up."

I pointed the rifle and squeezed the trigger. The sound of the shot rang across the meadow.

CHAPTER

18

I cannot forgive myself for what I did. It has long been one of my strictest principles not to interfere with the life of any individual, let alone attempt to shorten it. If an exception were to be made, Dr. Helvitius would surely qualify. It might be argued that, having neither scruples nor conscience, he had no claim upon the conscience of someone else—least of all, his intended victims. But that is a question to be resolved by a judgment higher than mine. In the event, my responsibility toward Vesper outweighed every other consideration.

I can state in all honesty: I meant only to wound him.

I cannot forgive myself—for missing the villain completely.

While my ears sang with the crack of the rifle shot, and smoke from the muzzle drifted through the air, Helvitius remained on his feet in front of me. I cursed my bad aim as much as I cursed my target. Helvitius smiled and made a mocking bow.

"Take them away." He swung astride his horse and spurred the animal up the trail without a backward glance, as if he had now entirely lost interest in us.

The rifle was snatched from my grasp before I could employ it further, the ruffians bound us hand and foot and flung us across their saddles as if we had been nothing more than inanimate bundles. I could not even communicate with Vesper to offer explanation or apology. Our captors led us, on separate mounts, at a brisk walking pace, back along the trail that once promised to be our path to freedom.

Vesper's surmise had been correct. Helvitius and his crew were familiar with the byways of this area, for our captors pressed on without difficulty although night had fallen. I expected them to return us to the *residencia.* Helvitius would not deny himself the pleasure of gloating over our failure before consigning us to some torment yet unknown.

To my bewilderment, they did not. Arriving at Corinto del Norte, we were borne not to the center of the ruined city but to the wharf. There, we were heaved like pieces of cargo into the bottom of a canoe or some other type of small boat.

"Dear girl," I murmured to Vesper at the first chance I had, "do they mean to drown us in the Culebra?"

"I doubt it," replied Vesper. "They'd have tossed us off the pier."

The boatmen continued plying their oars. My cramped position kept me from seeing over the gunwales, I was aware only of the lift and swell of the river. At last, with a jolt, the craft struck solid ground. Showing the same lack of humane concern, the oarsmen hauled us out, carried us between them a little distance, then dropped us into the undergrowth.

Vesper had been deposited a few feet away from me. In the moonlight, I saw her sit up. In an urgent whisper, I inquired if she had suffered any injury.

"I'm fine. No need to whisper, though. They've gone off and left us."

Above the night noises, I now detected the splash of oars. That sound soon died away. We had been abandoned.

With horror, the murderous villain's real plan became suddenly clear. Helvitius had given us over to the mercies of prowling animals or, worse, to the slow torture of scavenging insects or fire ants. Even before succumbing to thirst and hunger, we would be picked to the bone.

"Not right away, anyhow," said Vesper. "Roll closer, Brinnie. My fingers are a little numb, but I think I can do something about these ropes."

I did as she asked and felt the dear girl fumbling at my bonds. The knots held, Vesper muttered between her teeth and continued picking at them as best she could. Since we sat back to back in the darkness, her task would have been difficult enough. Clammy perspiration drenched us and her fingers often slipped uselessly over the cords.

"One end's loose," she cried at last, as I felt my bonds ease a little. "Work your wrists. Help me unwind the rope."

After a few moments, hands free, I devoted my energy to performing a similar service for Vesper. We lost no time unknotting the ropes binding our feet. Vesper stood up and groped through the bushes to the shore. Despite the moon's illumination, I saw only dark ripples at the water's edge and the Culebra glinting beyond.

Where they had marooned us I had no idea, nor had Vesper. She stood a while, taking stock of our surroundings, then turned back toward the undergrowth.

"No use crashing around in the dark," she said. "More than anything, we need a good sleep."

I heartily agreed. Though I marveled at how the dear girl could think of calm repose while our lives hung in the balance, we dared not exhaust ourselves in useless effort. It had been a trying day.

I blamed myself that we were prisoners once more. Through my inexcusably bad aim, Helvitius was triumphantly alive and we in his clutches.

"Dear girl," I sadly admitted, "I have failed you."

Vesper put her hand on my arm. "No, Brinnie," she replied, "there's no way you could ever fail me."

Such was our fatigue that only the full light of morning wakened us. While physically refreshed, I continued in spirits even lower than when we were recaptured. Vesper had put all vain regrets from her mind. She wanted breakfast.

"We won't starve. There must be fruits and berries for the picking. If we're thirsty, the Culebra has plenty of water."

She left me to my gloomy thoughts while she investigated the possibility of nourishment in the vicinity. Sunk in my ruminations, still blaming myself for our predicament, and seriously wondering if we would see our loved ones in Philadelphia again, I did not realize that some time had passed without a sign of the dear girl. I was about to go anxiously searching for her when she reappeared, arms filled with the abundant gifts of nature.

"We couldn't go hungry if we tried." Vesper offered me something like a variety of mango which, despite my lack of appetite, was agreeably tasty. "That makes me wonder about something else. Helvitius must have known we'd get loose of those ropes. He didn't care. I know why. He's got us nicely hemmed in."

At first, I thought she meant he had posted guards around us. Vesper shook her head.

"No need. We're not on the mainland. We're in the middle of the Culebra."

Vesper urged me to accompany her. As we skirted the shoreline, my heart fell. In the darkness of the previous night, I had not realized we had been flung into a worse prison cell: an island so small that Vesper assured me we could circle it in less than half an hour.

"If you hadn't been sitting there glooming," Vesper gently reproached me, "you'd have seen it as soon as I did." She pointed across the Culebra. "That's the riverbank opposite Corinto. It's not all that far. We could let the current carry us a good way downstream."

"Dear girl," I exclaimed, "you can't propose swimming."

"I'm not sure yet. It's worth a thought. I saw something else worth a thought, too."

We had, by now, come to the other side of the island. There, Vesper halted. I understood immediately what she meant. Although the expanse of river was much greater here, I could clearly make out the ruined wharves of Corinto and the *Midas* tied at one of the landing stages. At the end of a towrope from the stern of the larger vessel bobbed the little dinghy.

"We might not have to swim at all. Not too much, anyway. If we can get hold of that boat—"

Vesper chewed a thumbnail. "I don't know. It would be shorter swimming ashore, we'd be across the river and well away from Corinto. Then we'd have to hack our way overland, with Helvitius on our trail.

"He'll find out soon enough we've escaped," Vesper went on. "I'll bet he has someone with a telescope watching us from the harbor, on the opposite bank, too."

The villain would certainly have no scruples about intruding on our privacy. I suggested promptly withdrawing from sight.

"No hurry," said Vesper. "If we're being watched—they'll see we're stuck here, we're not trying to get away. That's what they'll see. But they can't hear us."

Vesper sat down by the water's edge and put her head in her hands. To any observer, the poor child was worn out and disconsolate. She continued, nevertheless, to examine our possibilities.

"Brinnie," she said finally, "We have to make a try for the dinghy. To start with, anyhow. What we need is a boat to carry us there."

"Dear girl," I broke in, "if we had such a thing—"

"We do," said Vesper. "That is, we will. When I was looking for food, I saw a lot of dead wood and branches. We can cobble them together with vines. It won't be much of a raft, but it's easier than swimming to the yacht. If we can steal the dinghy, so much the better. If not, we'll keep floating downstream as far as we can, then paddle ashore."

In my opinion, I told her, the scheme was foolhardy and dangerous.

"Of course it is," Vesper answered. "What else can we do? If we sit here, it'll be more than dangerous. It'll be fatal."

To this, I had no reply. I only hoped that Vesper's lucid intelligence had allowed her to weigh the decision carefully. In any case, I could offer no better alternative.

To avoid observation, we waited for nightfall. The day dragged, one of the longest in my life. Vesper occupied her time by strolling about the island, occasionally drifting toward its center. Her apparent idleness had a purpose. Bit by bit, she readied the materials we needed. When darkness came, we could quickly assemble our makeshift raft.

My apprehension grew as sundown approached and we made our way through the undergrowth to finish our work. I resigned myself, nevertheless, to whatever might befall. Better the perils of the river than any fate Helvitius had reserved for us.

We dragged our conveyance to the shore. Vesper, without hesitation, pushed off. I gritted my teeth and followed. While the Culebra in its lower reaches was a meandering tropical waterway, here the chill took my breath away and set me shuddering. Or, perhaps it was only a touch of nerves.

Clinging to the raft, which resembled a huge bird's nest more than floating vegetable matter, Vesper paddled with one arm as silently as she could. I did likewise, and our efforts gradually brought us to midstream. Under the moonless sky, the Culebra seemed wider than it had in sunlight—an expanse so endless that I began to fear we had passed the harbor. Vesper paddled steadily. After what felt like hours, I glimpsed the dark outline of the yacht and the trailing shadow of the dinghy. No lights shone from the portholes of the larger vessel, nor could I detect any illumination from the deck. Moments later, we were alongside. Vesper cast herself loose.

"Don't start rowing yet," she whispered before clambering over the gunwale. "Drift clear first. When they can't hear us, then row for all you're worth."

I heaved myself into the dinghy, which had begun to rock alarmingly. Vesper crawled forward to untie the line. I took hold of the oars, ready to ply them as soon as we were out of earshot. Vesper crawled back almost immediately.

"Brinnie—it's not a rope. A chain. Padlocked."

I stifled a gasp of despair. Vesper picked up one of the oars.

"We still have the raft. Take the other oar. We can use both of them."

She was about the climb back into the river when a lantern flared from the stern railing of the *Midas.* The orange glow turned the features of Dr. Helvitius more diabolical than usual as he grinned down at us. He raised his white yachting cap.

"Welcome aboard."

CHAPTER 19

What greater torment can there be for the wretched prisoner than the sweet taste of freedom turning suddenly to bitter ashes in his mouth? I shall not dwell on my own sensations of despair. Vesper's usually undaunted spirits had no doubt suffered more than mine. She said little, except for a few brief but scathing remarks in English and Spanish. The dear child had, I feared, fallen into mute hopelessness, which pained me even more than our unfortunate recapture.

Helvitius had given us the mariner's traditional greeting. Like all else about him, it was false. He did not welcome us aboard. He did not grant us so much as a moment's respite on his vessel. Instead, he watched with grim satisfaction as a rowboat pulled alongside the dinghy and we were forced to clamber into it. Our raft, by now, had floated away on the current. Had we the strength to wrestle free of our captors and dive overboard, we could not have sustained ourselves helpless in the river.

My mental anguish as great as my physical exhaustion,

my senses were so numbed that I paid no heed to our surroundings after we were taken ashore and flung into the bottom of a cart. My personal fate no longer interested me. My concern for Vesper alone kept me from lapsing into the relief of unconsciousness.

Thus, I was only dimly aware of being hauled from the jolting vehicle, rudely frog-marched into some shadowy structure, and thrust into what I had to believe were the confines of our last mortal remains.

Vesper stirred beside me. I heard her groping around in this lightless oubliette, and felt her hand on my face.

"There you are, Brinnie. I wasn't sure whether they tossed you in here head or feet first."

"The monster has entombed us!" I exclaimed. "Buried us alive!"

"Alive, but not buried." Vesper endeavored to take the measure of this new dungeon by feeling her way around the sides, knocking at one wall and another. Her head must have struck the low ceiling, for she gave a short cry. It was, however, not one of pain.

"Here it is. Boarded up. Yes, it would be. Come on, Brinnie, lend a shoulder. Push as hard as you can. They've blocked the regular entrance pretty solidly."

Too confused to question, I found the spot Vesper indicated. We shoved upward with all our strength. After several attempts, I heard the squeal of nails giving way and the splintering of wood.

At last, we stood upright. Though my eyes had grown more accustomed to the darkness, I saw only a wide, flat expanse before me and a sort of low canopy overhead.

"Too bad Madam Patti isn't on stage," Vesper said. "We'd have the best seats."

My mental distress had kept me from perceiving it. Helvitius, with delicate irony, had chosen to imprison us in the prompter's box of the Corinto opera house.

At how many brilliant performances had the humble prompter, crouched in his cubbyhole at the rim of the stage, peering out at the sopranos and tenors, whispered forgotten lines? Now the prompter himself was forgotten along with those he had so faithfully served. I put aside such reflections and started to crawl out.

"Not so fast," Vesper warned. "Lay low a bit. That's the best thing to do. Or maybe the worst."

Her words mystified me, as did her subsequent remarks.

"That dinner with Helvitius—it's been bothering me ever since."

"Dear girl, this is no time to dwell on his treachery. Whatever the blame, it is mine. If only I had shot him down in his tracks when I had the chance."

"You did, Brinnie," said Vesper. "In a way. I mean, it wasn't your fault. Think back. It all fits. What I don't understand is why I didn't catch on to it right away.

"He's going to kill us. No question about that," Vesper went on. "But what was it he said? It would depend on us? And what else did he say? *Au revoir.* He meant exactly that: He'd see us again. And so he did."

Vesper's mental processes raced swifter than my own sluggish thoughts as she continued.

"He could have had us killed right away. Why didn't he? He wanted his revenge, but he wanted to string it out and enjoy it, to amuse himself seeing what we'd do. He didn't drug us. He let us drug ourselves.

"We chose to drink that *chocolatl.* Were the cordials drugged, too? Suppose we'd taken the same brandy he did?

It wouldn't have mattered in the long run. He must have had some plan to match whatever we did.

"We thought we were making our own decisions. Well, I guess we were. We did the most logical and practical things: breaking out of the room, trying to steal the dinghy. That's what he counted on.

"When you shot at him, Brinnie, you didn't miss. You fired point-blank—*A quema ropa,* as Adelita says. The rifle had to be loaded with blank cartridges. The guard's bandolier, too, just in case you made off with it. Do you imagine Helvitius taking a chance with his own life? He was safe and he knew it.

"I'm not saying he figured out every detail. The details didn't make much difference. If we'd gone one direction instead of another, he'd have had some different way of catching us. He's been playing a game, Brinnie. A game he can't lose. Even if we do what seems right, it has to be wrong."

"This is the most monstrous trap of all!" I cried. "A trap of the spirit! He allowed us hope only to shatter it. Dear girl, you have understood his fiendish scheme—but we are lost whichever way we turn."

"Only if we play his game," said Vesper. "Only if we do what he expects us to do. Trouble with that," she added, "is figuring out what he expects—and not doing it. He put us in that room near the broken wall. He left us on the island in sight of the dinghy. Poisoned bait, Brinnie."

"But, dear girl, what if all the bait is poisoned?"

"Yes," Vesper said, "it probably is. He's had us on a string. He lets us go for a while before he pulls us back. We don't know how long the string is. And we don't know when he's going to end the game. Now? Here? Or does he still have more tricks up his sleeve?"

I put my hands to my head. My dear Mary—our prospects of seeing her again were dim at best. Our every move was tainted with the possibility that Helvitius had already foreseen it. Even now, he might be lurking in the shadows of the stage, waiting for us to emerge.

"We won't know until we try," said Vesper. "So far, he's guessed right. We have to make him start guessing wrong."

Helvitius, I pointed out, seemed able to guess our thoughts even before we shaped them. What we believed was right was wrong; what seemed wrong was likely wrong as well. Once, in Casablanca, Holly and I encountered a poor wretch who believed his brain had been turned inside out. I could sympathize.

"One thing he doesn't want," said Vesper, "is for us to come to serious harm. He's saving that to do himself. He'll keep us alive until he decides he wants us dead. If he thinks we're in danger—"

"We are in danger this very instant," I broke in. "What greater peril than sitting here waiting for him to strike?"

"At dinner, he said he controlled all the circumstances," replied Vesper. "We'll give him a circumstance he can't control."

During this, Vesper had been rummaging around the confines of the prompter's box. "I found what we need. Did Helvitius put them here on purpose?"

She pressed a waxy, cylindrical object into my hand: I realized it was a candle.

"I found some more," Vesper said. "I doubt that they're

a gift from Helvitius. The prompter had to have light so he could follow the opera libretto. These must have been left when the opera was abandoned. Here's a box of old lucifer matches, too. If they still work, we have a chance."

Vesper clambered out and crouched on the apron of the stage. The first match broke and crumbled in her fingers, the next few only flared briefly. She persisted until one flamed long enough to light one candle, and we lit the others from it.

"A good big fire should do it," said Vesper. "I don't like burning down opera houses. It makes me feel like Attila the Hun. But this one's ruined anyway. Look around for curtains, drapes, scenery, anything like that."

"Of course!" I could, again, only marvel at the dear girl's agile intelligence. Her plan was dazzling in its classical simplicity. "Once the hall's aflame, we make a dash—"

"No, Brinnie," said Vesper. "Just the opposite. We stay. I'm betting Helvitius has guards watching the building. They'll see us come out. So, we wait until the last moment. If Helvitius thinks we're in real danger, he'll make sure we're rescued. He'll send his people in to save us. Once they're inside searching for us—that's when we run for it."

What, I wondered, if he decided to let us burn?

"I suppose," Vesper said, "we'll soon find out."

Ruined as it was, Corinto's once-glorious opera house proved to be a huge tinderbox. With lighted candles, we sped through the backstage maze of dressing rooms, costume closets, racks of moldering canvas backdrops. The flames spread so rapidly I feared we might be engulfed in the very blaze we were setting.

The fire swept through the main hall, roaring as if all the long departed audiences had returned to fill the house with spectral ovations, and the leaping flames burned brighter than ever the antique footlights had done.

Vesper's plan, in short, succeeded beyond our wildest hopes—and nearly succeeded all too well. We crouched in a recess at the end of a passage near the stage entrance. Smoke had begun to stifle us, the flames licked closer along the walls.

I had just about decided we had done the villain's work for him by letting ourselves burn to a crisp when a pair of guards burst through the stage door. They raced by our hiding place to join their fellows who had entered the main hall. I heard them shouting to each other, and, above the crackling, the furious voice of Helvitius.

"Find them! They must be here. I want them alive!"

Vesper climbed to her feet. "Brinnie, it's time to leave."

CHAPTER 20

Behind us, flames rolled upward from the blazing building, staining the clouds and screening the mountain slopes with a billowing crimson curtain. I still marveled at our escape with injuries no greater than disagreeable but minor blisters where sparks had eaten through our clothing. Vesper's hair had been a little singed, but she disregarded this mishap as we picked our way through Corinto's back streets and narrow *callejuelas.*

My tendency had been for us to take to our heels and sprint for dear life. Vesper held me back.

"Just move along quietly," she whispered. "Run and we'll catch someone's eye. Helvitius has most of his people trying to put out the fire, but we don't know who else could be hanging around." She glanced over her shoulder. "Not likely he'll rebuild the opera house now. Too bad. I'd have liked to hear Madam Patti."

From what I glimpsed, the ill-fated building had indeed undergone a second destruction worse than the first. More than that, the fire which had been our salvation showed signs of spreading to the *residencia* of Helvitius. He would, thanks to Vesper, be a very busy man for some while. I also realized that the pinkish hue of the sky came not only from the fire. We had little time before it would be full daylight.

Calmly and steadily, Vesper headed in the direction of the old harbor. The landing stage lay deserted, as far as we could judge. Helvitius had no doubt pressed every man into a vain attempt to extinguish the fire. We halted and clung to the shadows of a ruined wall. The yacht, we saw, had docked and was tied at the wharf.

"No use going for the dinghy again," said Vesper. "Still, I wonder—"

Vesper has never hesitated to think in the largest terms. There was an unmistakable glint in her eye as she studied the vessel. She sighed and shook her head.

"Better not chance it. Some of the crew might still be aboard. We could end up in worse trouble. It's tempting, though. What a facer for Helvitius. That's one thing he wouldn't expect."

I felt relieved when she turned away reluctantly, and we crept stealthily to the water's edge.

"They brought us here in a rowboat," Vesper murmured. "It must be around somewhere."

She clambered cautiously down a flight of wooden steps to the remains of a sagging pier. The boat had been moored alongside. With a hasty glance around to make sure we were not observed—at least as far as we could determine—Vesper stepped aboard.

"They left the oars," she whispered. "That's a piece of

luck. Cast off, Brinnie. It's not much for style, but we'll make do with it."

We bobbed silently into the Culebra as the sun broke through the low-hanging clouds. Vesper unshipped the oars. The current aided our efforts at rowing and the small craft slid quickly downstream. This time, we had truly slipped through the scoundrel's fingers.

Or had we?

This idea haunted me even as Corinto disappeared in our wake. As Vesper had said, Helvitius held us on a string. Each time, he had let us go a little further before snatching us back. Had we escaped him or had he merely lengthened our tether?

"He's the only one who knows," Vesper said. "Don't wait around to ask him."

Robust though she was, our ordeals of the past days had taken their toll on the dear child. We had gone sleepless and without food for what felt like at least eighty years. Vesper's face was drawn with fatigue, it looked narrow and pinched under the smudges of soot. Even so, she resisted the temptation to row ashore and seek food and rest. We took turns at the oars, allowing each other some respite.

During my stint, Vesper curled up in the stern and promptly dozed off. We had agreed to rouse each other every half hour, by our closest reckoning. I had no heart to disturb the dear girl and continued past my allotted time.

By now, the sun beat down directly upon us from a cloudless sky. After some while, the stinging heat ceased to be disagreeable as I fell comfortably into the monotonous rhythm of dipping the oars, stroke after stroke. Instead of the Culebra, it seemed to me that I was home again, sculling along the pleasant reaches of our delightful Schuylkill River; a happy scene, much like those that one of Holly's friends—a local artist of modest talent—had been so fond of painting. The fellow's name eluded me: Adkin, Atkins, or some such.

Next thing I knew, Vesper was shaking me by the shoulders.

"Eakins!" I exclaimed. "Tom Eakins!"

"Brinnie, wake up! What are you mumbling about?"

Vesper snatched the oars. The Schuylkill vanished. Our little boat spun in the current of the Culebra, my feet awash up to my ankles.

"Leaking fast," Vesper muttered between her teeth as she pulled hard for shore. By the time she righted our craft and sent us crashing into the tangle of roots and creepers at the riverbank, we had taken on a fair amount of water.

"We could try to plug the bottom with twigs, moss, whatever's around," said Vesper, after we had tipped over the boat and drained it. "That wouldn't help much. We'd still have to keep bailing."

She shaded her eyes to look across the expanse of water. "No way to guess, Brinnie. Helvitius didn't find our bodies. He knows we're on the loose, and he must know we took the boat. So, I say let's get rid of it now. If he thinks we're sailing downstream, so much the better. If he does find the boat, we won't be on it."

We righted the little craft and shoved it into the current. With some regret, I watched the river catch at it and carry it out of sight.

"At least he won't know where we landed," said Vesper. "Come on, Brinnie, our ride's over. It's feet from now on."

What goaded us beyond our strength was our constant fear that Helvitius and his ruffians would all too accurately guess the direction we had taken. As we struggled through heavy undergrowth for the rest of that day, I strained my ears for any sound of footfalls behind us. Night, when we were forced to rest, proved worse, for each jungle noise, however harmless, brought us bolt upright. Vesper had insisted on taking the oars as a makeshift means of defense. Privately, I doubted they would be much use against rifles —rifles, this time, that would not be loaded with blank cartridges.

After another long day and, for me, an equally long and nervous night, Vesper turned from the riverbank and headed a little inland.

"We'll reach Ocotalpa sooner than the village," she said. "Acharro gave his people instructions at the lake before we—before we lost him. If they've kept on with the work there, we'll be in friendly hands."

Vesper, by now, had grown more confident of outdistancing Helvitius. This belief did not raise her spirits. Rather, she turned silent and unusually downcast. Her thoughts, I realized, had returned to Acharro. Nothing I could say cheered her as we trudged on, venturing over more open and easier paths. The forest canopy parted as we crossed a little savannah. Vesper halted in her tracks.

"They've started!" She pointed toward the green foothills beyond us. Distant but clearly visible, from the crest of Ocotalpa rose a black thread of smoke.

"They've lit some torches. They should use more. It's good. Not good enough yet—but they're doing it!"

With renewed energy, she set off across the grassy belt, eager to pass through the forest and reach the uplands with all haste.

They found us then.

I had, in Afghanistan, seen a hundred tribesmen spring from what I would have sworn to be the barest rock face. Here, even more startling, forms burst from the shrubbery before my eyes. I swung up the oar I had been shouldering and prepared to fend off our attackers.

"You won't need that," said Vesper.

Suncha ran toward us. Behind her followed Ita and a dozen or more village women.

"We have searched up and down both riverbanks," cried Suncha, embracing Vesper. "Caymans, Jaguars, all of us. Some feared you were past finding, but Acharro kept our hopes up."

"Acharro?" Vesper's face brightened. "He's alive?"

The tall figure of the chieftain was already pressing through the crowd of villagers.

"They left me for dead. An assumption that was almost correct." Acharro held out his arms and Vesper greeted him with less formality than a chieftain might have demanded. It did not appear to trouble him. Vesper waved away his questions, promising a full account later.

"The important thing is you did it," she hurried on. "The torches are perfect. Maybe just a little more smoke—"

"The whole village has been looking for you since the ambush," Acharro broke in. "What you see is not our work. Ocotalpa has come alive again."

CHAPTER

21

I will not go so far as to say Acharro's words astonished Vesper as they did me. Learning that a volcano, certifiably extinct, has suddenly become active, would give anyone pause; all the more when it might erupt momentarily. Even as Acharro spoke, the thread of smoke thickened into a heavy black column. The dear girl, I realized, was not so much taken aback as disappointed.

"Yes, well, it does save us climbing around," she said, after observing the spreading cloud for several moments. "Still, we could have put on as good a show."

To my dismay, she now proposed heading closer to Ocotalpa. "It's my volcano, after all. If it blows, I want to see it."

This, Acharro refused to allow. I added my own disapproval and reminded her that Dr. Helvitius would not have given up looking for us with rancor added to his lust for revenge. When I briefly told Acharro what the vile fiend had attempted, his face set in hard lines.

"Leave us to deal with him." Acharro took Vesper's arm. "I did not find you only to lose you. My father has the *Libertador* in a backwater not far from here. He has been following along with us should we need his boat.

"As we do now," Acharro added. "He and I will go with you to Puerto Palmas. We shall make certain you are safely aboard the first ship outward bound—for Jamaica, Cuba, no matter where, as long as you are away from El Dorado. My Chiricas will see to it that Helvitius never threatens you again."

He smiled fondly at Vesper. "You have my word. We shall not attack the work camp. It will not be necessary. Ocotalpa has settled matters. De Rochefort will not dare keep on with the canal.

"Your plan worked without you, but you kept us from destroying ourselves. There is nothing greater, and nothing more, that you can do."

"I have something else in mind," said Vesper.

Acharro declined to hear more. He instructed Suncha, Ita, and the others to return to the village, board canoes to cross the river, and call in the remainder of the search party.

Vesper should have felt relieved as Acharro led us to join Blazer. She did not. She must have sensed, as I did, the strange atmosphere fallen over the jungle. Birds chattered in more than usual agitation. Monkeys scurried among the trees, and we often caught sight of small animal forms darting through the bushes.

"They feel Ocotalpa's heartbeat," said Acharro. "Or, if you prefer, stresses in the substrata which accompany volcanic activity—"

He broke off and motioned us to halt. From a break in

the undergrowth, a sleek black jaguar had appeared. The magnificent animal paused an instant, fixing us with glowing eyes. Vesper caught her breath and stared in admiration at the powerful creature. The jaguar made a sound that was half growl, half murmur, and vanished into the bush.

Acharro had suddenly grown troubled. "The animals know more than we do. They sense the earth is restless. We must reach the *Libertador* with all speed."

"I don't know about the animals," said Vesper, "but I feel a little odd, too. Something's going on."

I hastened to assure them both that it was surely no impending earthquake. I reminded Vesper: The most expert scientific opinion had established, beyond the shadow of a doubt, that no such event could occur.

Next moment, I was flat on my back. The ground seemed to have lurched and sent me sprawling. I have seldom felt more disoriented and, frankly, terrified. I could scarcely collect my wits. Acharro was shouting at us to hurry. Vesper ran toward me.

It was then that a clump of bushes and the nearest trees pitched askew with horrifying groaning and grinding noises. Acharro, barely dodging a falling tree trunk, had tumbled amid the branches. And Vesper—the dear girl had disappeared.

The air itself rippled before my eyes. It took me an instant to realize that a jagged fissure had opened and Vesper had stumbled into it. The child was trying to claw her way upward, but the ground fell away under her hands.

"Brinnie, no! Don't try it!"

By then, paying no heed to her warning, I had already leaped into the gaping trench and seized her around the waist. In one burst of strength, I heaved her out, well past the rim, and staggered back against the earthen wall.

Acharro was at the edge. He and Vesper gripped my outstretched arms and plucked me free. Acharro did not give us a moment to catch our breath or congratulate each other on a narrow escape.

"This is only the first shock," he cried, pressing us on as fast as we could go. "There will be others."

Behind me, I heard more rumblings and the crash of falling trees. I did not care to look back. My worst fear was that—contrary to the geologists' opinion—the fault lines might extend to the river bed. We would have to contend with a flood as well as an earthquake. The *Libertador* could be shattered into matchwood and all aboard swept away. The scientific experts, I reluctantly had to admit, could have been more thorough in their work.

Thanks to Acharro's unerring guidance, we at last reached the inlet. Blazer had been beside himself with worry. He hustled us aboard the *Libertador,* bawled for Slider to cast off; then, once in midstream, he gave us such a bone-cracking welcome that I feared we had escaped the earthquake only to be squashed by Blazer. The tremors, in any case, had ceased for the time being. My heart still pounded, but Vesper had put our harrowing flight from her thoughts and had turned her attention to reaching Puerto Palmas.

"*Mavourneen,*" said Blazer when we were sufficiently out of danger to relax, and Vesper had given him an account of the happenings in Corinto, "I wish I could have been there to lay hands on that pair of villains. No matter. You've settled them once and for all."

"Not by half," said Vesper. "It'll do for the time being."

Adelita, meanwhile, had flapped down from wherever she had been roosting and made directly for me, squawking and whistling. Though I could have done without her nips and impudent comments, I was glad to see her. I preferred her company to that of Helvitius and his treacherous hireling.

Blazer piloted the *Libertador* downstream, exuberantly blasting away on the whistle. Vesper and Acharro stayed with him in the pilothouse while Slider—or Smiler—worked at the boilers to build up a good head of steam. For myself, I was grateful to find my old quarters in the texas and stretch out there under Adelita's watchful eye.

By my reckoning, we had only begun to swing around the curve of the oxbow, with Acharro's village still some distance away, when the *Libertador* lurched and shuddered. I hurried out onto the deck. The paddle wheel had stopped and Blazer was stamping around in a fine state of aggravation.

Vesper tried to calm him. "It's probably the vent, same as before. I showed Smiler what to do."

This, alas, was not the case. Smiler himself soon came up from the engine room to report one of the piston rods had broken loose.

"Then fix it, bedad!" Blazer's temper rose in the same degree that our steam pressure fell. Vesper offered her engineering services, but, before she set foot on the ladder, Slider scrambled up, his genial moon face eclipsed by alarm.

"Ship astern," he told Blazer. "Just come round the bend. I didn't sight her till now."

Blazer snatched a telescope and ran to see for himself. Neither Vesper nor I needed such an instrument to recognize the oncoming vessel.

"The *Midas.*" Vesper's voice was even, but the dear girl's features tensed and her eyes narrowed. "I wonder if Helvitius is aboard."

"There's a big fellow in the bow," said Blazer, "with a spyglass watching me watching him. I'd wager he's seen us all. Too late to hide, *macushlah.*"

Though it was, no doubt, Smiler's line of work, Slider hurried below to help his twin. Vesper, too, would have gone, but Acharro declared there was no time for repairs.

"Lower your lifeboat," Acharro told Blazer. "We still have a chance to row ashore."

"Lifeboat, is it?" cried Blazer. "She'll sink with all hands, the bottom's rotted out. I never saw the use for one —till now."

"Can you drift us closer to land?" Acharro demanded. "Near enough for us to swim?"

Blazer had no time to answer. Driven by its powerful propeller, the steam yacht was closing upon us at full speed. We flung ourselves to the deck as a volley of shots tore through the *Libertador*'s superstructure, smashing the windows of the pilothouse and splintering the railings.

"The devils!" roared Blazer. "I know a Gatling gun when I hear it!"

Apart from the whoops and ululations of maddened dervishes, the trumpeting of wild elephants, and the terrifying rebel yell, few sounds are more unnerving than the deadly stutter of this deplorable invention of Mr. Richard Gatling. How I wished he had confined his talents to beneficial agricultural implements, instead of this mechanical gun with its rotating barrel spewing an endless hail of bullets.

"Rifles!" cried Acharro. "We can hold our own for a little while."

"Dear boy, they're all in the village." Blazer groaned. "Not a one left aboard."

Defense, in any case, would have been useless. With the dreadful Gatling gun still firing upon us, the yacht implacably drew alongside. When the awful fusillade ceased, and we dared to raise our heads, a plank had already been run out from the *Midas* to the helpless *Libertador.*

While the two ruffians who had been cranking and feeding the gun kept this weapon trained upon us, another band, rifles at the ready, strode across the plank. Following them came de Rochefort, revolver in hand, and his despicable master.

"Bloody pirates!" Blazer shook his fist. "Bloody murdering ditchdiggers!"

"Be silent, you dissolute Hibernian. You are of no importance to me." Helvitius turned a scornful glance on Acharro. "Nor is this *indio* and the rest of his savages. Whatever satisfaction it may give you to know that I shall terminate my work on the canal, I wish you the joy of it."

Helvitius now faced Vesper and me. "Your land, Miss Holly, is worthless for my purposes. Contrary to all expert evaluations, the volcano is not extinct. Alain assures me, and I accept it, that my project must be abandoned. I leave Corinto del Norte, and El Dorado, with personal regrets—but in the certain knowledge that I shall find other endeavors worthy of my attention.

"There remains only one matter to be settled," Helvitius went on. "Your intelligence, Miss Holly, is almost equal to my own. You have by now surely perceived that I chose to amuse myself with you and Professor Garrett. I no longer have time nor interest in prolonging my little game. It is over.

"I confess I did not expect to find you aboard this pitiful vessel, but I shall not forgo the opportunity good fortune has brought me." He turned to de Rochefort. "Alain, before we depart, please perform one service for me. Shoot them both."

CHAPTER

22

Vesper did not deign to give Helvitius so much as a glance, let alone a reply. She addressed herself, rather, to de Rochefort.

"I'm really sorry for you." Vesper looked him squarely in the face with such calm strength of spirit that any Philadelphian would, like myself, have admired her. It surprised me that the Frenchman had the courage to meet her gaze. "Honor? Noblesse? You're not a pelican. You're a jellyfish."

If Vesper expected her comments to sway him, the dear girl for once had erred in her judgment. De Rochefort showed not the slightest trace of shame or regret. Why she bandied words with him at all seemed a waste of what few moments of life remained to us.

Then I realized she was far from resigned to our fate. As she continued to express her opinion, from the corner of my eye I glimpsed the yacht and the *Libertador* slowly drifting downstream ever closer to the riverbank. Poor child! She was pinning her last hope on leaping overboard and swimming to shore. Vain delusion! We would be shot down before we could take a step toward the railing.

"I cannot expect your opinion of me to change, Mademoiselle Holly," de Rochefort replied. "Nevertheless, tarnished beyond repair, my honor has not entirely ceased to guide me. Not in a courageous path, but one most available."

De Rochefort turned now to Helvitius. "This is the best occasion to enlighten you and to answer the question you raised concerning the volcano. The evidence of your own eyes tells you, and quite correctly, it is not extinct.

"What you do not know is this: It never was."

"My map says it is," Vesper put in. "Your geologists surveyed it. They told you it was dead."

"No," answered de Rochefort. "Your map is outdated and inaccurate. As for the geologists, their reports to me stated beyond question: The volcano was active and could erupt at any time. Their studies also warned me of danger from severe earthquakes. The fault lines precisely follow the route of the canal."

"What are you saying, you fool?" burst out Helvitius. "I myself examined those studies."

"So you thought. You did not see the original surveys. You saw the ones I rewrote and changed. It was I who falsified them.

"I did so deliberately," de Rochefort continued. "I wished you to believe that nothing could threaten your project."

"You are insane." The face of Helvitius went white beneath his tan. "You are not only a thief but a madman."

"Far from it," said de Rochefort. "You forced me to serve you. In that, I had no better choice. Did you suppose I could tolerate that vile slavery?

"I promised myself revenge. I was patient, willing to bide my time. Sooner or later, I knew that Ocotalpa would destroy what you accomplished."

"As I shall destroy you, my dear Alain," said Helvitius.

"You have already done that. What happens to me is of no importance. I have had my revenge.

"One portion of it," de Rochefort added. "I have yet another account to settle and I shall do that now. You humiliated me in the eyes of Mademoiselle Holly. You stripped away the last shred of my mask of self-respect. Until then, I would have been content to let time and nature shatter your ambitions. Now, I shall be satisfied with nothing less than your life."

De Rochefort turned away the revolver he had been pointing at us and leveled it at Helvitius.

"Do not kill him," said Helvitius. "I shall have him alive." He made a slight motion toward one of the ruffians standing behind the Frenchman. Before de Rochefort could pull the trigger, the man swung his rifle butt down on his head. De Rochefort staggered and fell to the deck.

At a further command from Helvitius, his henchmen aimed their weapons at us.

"Count yourselves fortunate to die so quickly," said Helvitius. "Alain will envy you."

"You might envy *him,*" said Vesper. She had been facing Helvitius squarely with an air of calm courage that set an example for us all. Now her gaze went past him as she added, "I think you have visitors."

I did not comprehend her meaning. But Helvitius, startled, had taken a backward step. Before he could order his men to fire, a number of figures sprang upon them. I was, at first, too bewildered to realize who they were, so swiftly and silently had they come.

"Suncha!" cried Vesper. "Ita!"

The village women were aboard the *Libertador.*

Armed with canoe paddles, Suncha and her companions flailed right and left among our captors. The guards, so taken unawares, found themselves suddenly being battered into disarray. Astonished and dismayed, they could only strive to escape the ferocious assault.

"Lend me that." Vesper caught up a paddle from one of the women and, her face alight, set about belaboring Helvitius. The wretch flung up his hands to fend her off, then spun away from her vigorous blows. Acharro, at the same time, sprang to the aid of Ita and sent one of the ruffians crashing into the railing. Blazer joyfully threw himself into the fray, bellowing at the top of his voice. Smiler—or Slider—materialized close at hand.

As fate would have it, I found myself confronting the guard I had felled in Corinto. The wretch must have borne me a personal grudge. Deprived of his weapon, he attempted to throttle me with his bare hands.

In Shanghai, an old master of *tai-chi chuan* had instructed Holly and me in the rudiments of this formidable defensive art. I quickly assumed the attitude called "Step Back and Repel Monkey." Had I been in better practice, I would surely have had the fellow's life on my conscience. My maneuver proved less than effective. My head swam as the wretch persisted in choking the breath out of me.

"¡A quema ropa! ¡Fuego!"

Hearing this bloodchilling command, certain that he was being attacked at point-blank range, my opponent released me and whirled around. Adelita, squawking and jabbering, swooped upon him, flapping her wings and nipping at him with her fearsome beak.

Helvitius, dodging Vesper's assault, raced over the plank to seek protection aboard the *Midas.* His henchmen were at his heels. My assailant, fighting off Adelita, darted after them.

Vesper, quite certainly, would have led the village women to pursue the villainous doctor. At that instant, however, the *Libertador* suddenly lurched ahead. The plank sheered away as our paddle wheel churned into motion. While his twin had come to aid us, Slider—or Smiler—had completed repairs to the piston and set our craft sailing down the Culebra.

Blazer ran to take the helm. Vesper joyfully embraced Suncha and Ita.

"A minute later," she told them, "and we wouldn't have been in any condition to welcome you aboard."

Acharro had still not overcome his astonishment. He looked at the Chirican women as if seeing them now for the first time. "I owe my life to you. That is a debt greater than even a chief can repay."

"Not necessarily," put in Vesper. "But, for now, I'm wondering how Suncha and the others found us."

"We had taken canoes, as Acharro ordered," replied Suncha, "and had gone to call in the Caymans and Jaguars. Coming back, we saw the *Libertador* and knew you were in peril. We tied our canoes alongside and climbed aboard. The rest was not too difficult."

"Don't be so modest," said Vesper. "You saved us from Helvitius. That isn't easy, as I well know."

We were, however, by no means out of danger. As we pulled away from the yacht, the Gatling gun commenced its dreadful chatter. Led by one of the twins, some of the women raced down the ladder to the engine room, hoping to stoke the boilers and increase our steam pressure.

It was a futile effort. For a little while, the *Libertador* indeed outdistanced the *Midas.* Blazer steered as close to shore as he dared, counting on the larger vessel to stay off in midstream. The enraged Helvitius, flinging caution to the winds, bore down upon us ever more swiftly. Bullets rattled through the *Libertador*'s smokestack, the incessant volleys threatened to shatter the paddle wheel itself.

I could almost hear the triumphant shout of Helvitius as he strove to board us again or run us down. With no more than canoe paddles and a few hastily abandoned rifles, we prepared to face one last and surely fatal engagement as the yacht steadily gained upon us.

What I saw, then, convinced me that my senses had been deranged. Vesper confirmed the reality of what I thought was hallucination.

"The yacht!" she cried. "It's heading into the riverbank! No—Brinnie, the riverbank's heading into the yacht!"

It was true, though I could scarcely believe my eyes. As Acharro predicted, the earthquake had struck again, this time, with an effect even more powerful. A whole portion of the riverbank to our stern had risen up and detached itself from the mainland.

With a roar that made the firing of the Gatling gun no more than a feeble crackling, a wall of earth, uprooted trees, and giant boulders flung up from hidden depths appeared to hang poised in midair. For those few seconds, it seemed to me that the shoreline had gone topsy-turvy. Tree trunks leaned crazily, the jungle floor tilted so that even as I watched I could not be sure that the horizon itself had not shifted.

Then, with a deafening roar, what once had been solid ground crashed like an avalanche into the Culebra.

It caught the *Midas* broadside, snatched at its keel, and sent the vessel listing so sharply that its masts nearly plunged into the water. Propeller still spinning madly in empty air, the vessel lay stranded amid the tangle of tree trunks and huge clumps of undergrowth.

"Gone aground!" cried Vesper. "They're stuck like flies in molasses!"

She ran to the pilothouse. The dear girl, I sincerely believe, would have wished to go back and capture the stranded Helvitius. Fearing the *Libertador* might share the fate of the *Midas,* Blazer wisely sailed ahead full speed, leaving Helvitius to the mercy of the aftershocks.

Nearing Acharro's village, the wounded *Libertador* could go no further. With much clanking and grinding, the laboring engine expired and the paddle wheel creaked to a halt. The Chirican men had, by now, sighted us from shore. They launched canoes and paddled hurriedly to our disabled vessel.

Whether the first to climb aboard was a Cayman or a Jaguar, I do not know. Either way, he was an extremely surprised Chirica as he found himself face to face with the village women.

"We're glad to see you," said Suncha, "but we've already done most of the work—as usual."

Ita and the other women joined in with similar comments. It was, I am sure, mostly good-natured teasing and raillery, with a great deal of laughter—from the women. As for the Caymans and Jaguars, I do not know if it was their custom to blush and look sheepish, but, on that occasion, they did both.

Suncha rightly claimed the honor of ferrying us ashore. The women's canoes had remained undamaged, Blazer flung down a rope ladder and helped Ita remove the still unconscious de Rochefort.

Vesper, Acharro, and I were handed into Suncha's canoe. As she and her companions made for shore, Vesper, disregarding the rules of seamanship—as she disregards so many others—chose to stand upright in the bow, in a striking resemblance to Herr Leutze's notable depiction of Washington crossing the Delaware.

Before we landed, the sky darkened though it was hardly close to nightfall. From the distance came a low rumbling that grew louder each moment. The women ceased paddling and turned their eyes toward the barely visible line of hills.

I braced myself for another tremor.

"Not this time," said Acharro. "It is Ocotalpa. He has been silent, these years. Now he speaks to us again."

As we watched, an explosion mightier than a dozen thunderclaps rent the air. A massive column of orange and crimson rose and spread in a fountain of flames. The eruption gained in strength as bombs of molten lava burst skyward from the heart of the volcano.

I could only stare in mute reverence. I took the occasion privately to contemplate the frailty of human creatures before the awesome and overwhelming forces of nature. Vesper, at last, broke the silence that had fallen over all of us.

"That," she said, "is even better than I could have done."

CHAPTER 23

Vesper is no stranger to public acclamation. She accepts ovations, torchlight parades, triumphal processions, and similar displays with unfailing graciousness—on condition they do not last too long. Since the village population was small, her welcome was limited in scope but not enthusiasm. Only one thing marred the happy occasion. Some of the Chiricas had gone to the stranded *Midas* and found it deserted. Helvitius had apparently disappeared beyond pursuit into the jungle.

"Blast him, Brinnie!" she burst out. "He's slipped through our fingers."

I reminded her that we were the ones who had slipped through *his* fingers. She was still far from satisfied, but had more pressing matters to take up with Acharro.

"I'd like you to call a tribal council," she told him. "I said they'd listen to me next time. And this is next time."

Acharro willingly agreed. He summoned his Caymans and Jaguars to his *residencia* the following day. The meeting was much like the one we had first attended: the same crowd of warriors, the same elders in ceremonial garb. This time, I observed, they looked noticeably pleasanter than before. There was no grumbling about Vesper's presence. In fact, they greeted her with warmest cheers.

Vesper thanked them, then looked around, puzzled. She turned to Acharro.

"I thought," she said, "this was going to be a tribal meeting."

"So it is," he replied, "as I promised you."

"You forgot something," said Vesper. "I expected you might. Don't worry, I've seen to it. A tribal meeting means all the tribe, not just half."

At this, there was a sudden commotion in the back of the room. The elders sprang to their feet, the warriors turned to stare openmouthed at the doorway.

Suncha, Ita, and all the village women surged into the council chamber.

I could not determine whether Caymans or Jaguars were shouting in greater astonishment. I scored it a tie, and judged them to be equally taken aback. Indeed, it required the combined efforts of Acharro and Vesper to produce any kind of order.

"They have every right to be here," declared Vesper. "For one thing, they saved your chief. For another—well, they're Chiricas, like all of you."

"This is true." Acharro had come to stand beside Vesper. "Until now, it has not been our custom. But our custom no longer serves us. How it began, or by whom, is long forgotten. It is ended."

"You have a new custom, that's all," Vesper said. "After a little while, it will be an old custom. You'll even start to like it."

There was still some scandalized muttering here and there. Vesper ignored it and continued, "The first thing I want to tell all of you is simply this: There's no way your land can really belong to me. Your ancestors are buried here, not mine. I can't own them and never could. As soon as I can, I'll ask Kenge and Carboy to untangle the red tape. I just wanted you to know it now. I'm turning over my property here to the Chiricas—to all the Chiricas, men and women alike.

"There's something else, too. When Acharro and I were talking about handicrafts, he said you couldn't make enough of them to matter. That's not quite true. You can."

"You may specialize in the impossible," Acharro broke in, "but there is a limit to what our women can do."

"By themselves, yes," Vesper said. "Not if the Caymans and Jaguars work along with them. They can learn if they put their minds to it. It won't hurt them to make themselves useful."

"What are you saying?" sputtered one of the elders. "Are you asking men to do women's work?"

"If they do it," said Vesper, "it won't be women's work anymore. It will be everybody's. You'll all build your own kind of El Dorado, and a nice little one it should be."

Acharro grinned and shook his head. "I cannot refute your logic—"

"You don't have to," said Vesper.

I would be less than truthful if I portrayed the rest of the meeting as unanimous agreement. There was, at first, a certain amount of indignation among the Caymans and Jaguars. In the end, however, the women carried the day. The warriors accepted Vesper's plan and, at Acharro's urging, promised to do their best. To console themselves at the prospect of going to work, they declared yet another celebration for the following night.

On that occasion, we were named honorary Chiricas. The village women presented Vesper with one of their magnificent costumes, and me with an ornamented *taparrabo.* This gift I accepted more as a token than a practical garment, but Vesper insisted on my wearing it. After I got used to it I did find it comfortable and, if I may say so, not unbecoming.

While Ocotalpa continued rumbling, its voice never matched the spectacular display of the first eruption, and the volcano soon lapsed into silence. The village lay far enough away to escape damage from lava and ash. The earthquake, however, had not entirely spared the Chiricas. The palisade had tumbled, some of the huts had been leveled. These, thanks to their construction of flexible rattan and thatch, could be repaired in short order. Of more concern to Acharro was the diversion of a spring which had been the main supply of fresh water.

As Vesper and Acharro studied ways to solve this problem, Blazer and the twins revived the *Libertador.* Suncha, Ita, and the other women took turns caring for the injured de Rochefort, an example of kindness and charity I could only admire.

When the Frenchman had sufficiently recovered, Acharro summoned him to the *residencia* to decide his fate. Vesper and I were present that afternoon when de Rochefort arrived, looking somewhat the worse for wear and, understandably, rather apprehensive about his future.

"I'm sorry you got hit on the head," Vesper told him, "but I hope it knocked some sense into you. There must be some way you can go back and straighten things out. Let Helvitius do his worst. You can't keep running away forever."

"I do not wish to run," said de Rochefort. "I hope I may be allowed to stay where I am. I am a skilled engineer. There are many things I can do here. I can recover the water supply, for one. Also, I can improve the looms and pottery wheels. With help from the village people, I can salvage the yacht. The Chiricas or *le capitaine* O'Hara shall be able to use it for their own purposes."

"I do not deny your value to us," Acharro said. "But I must tell you this: We do not often welcome strangers to stay among us. It is our custom, if one wishes to do so, for a Chirica to speak on his behalf. Failing that, it is not possible."

"I understand." De Rochefort bowed his head. "I cannot expect such a favor. I shall leave your village as soon as I am able to travel."

"Hold on," put in Vesper. "I'm a Chirica now. I'll speak for him."

"You have that right," said Acharro. "The decision is yours, then. Do you permit him to stay?"

"As long as he wants," replied Vesper. She turned to de Rochefort. "I called you a jellyfish. I'm not taking that back, because that's what you were. At the time. Since then, you've turned out to be a pretty good sort of pelican."

After de Rochefort gratefully left us, Acharro took Vesper's hands in his own. "It is our custom to speak the truth. I must do so now. I have, after much careful thought, come to this conclusion: There is none other in the world like Miss Vesper Holly."

Vesper pondered this a while, on her face that expression of innocent candor and girlish modesty which I have always found so endearing.

"You're probably right," said Vesper.

Our return voyage merits no extended account. I shall only note that Blazer and the twins, with Adelita impudent as ever, sailed us to Puerto Palmas on the refurbished *Libertador.* Acharro, Suncha, and de Rochefort accompanied us. Dressed as we were, our arrival at our hotel raised eyebrows among guests and staff. Though we retrieved our baggage, Vesper preferred to wear her Chirican garb. I changed into my travel clothing, feeling that my tribal membership did not extend beyond the borders of El Dorado.

We did not reach Philadelphia in the same luxury with which we left it. The *City of Brotherly Love* would not stop in Puerto Palmas for some weeks. Acharro urged us to stay, but our trip had already been too long extended. We took passage on the first available transportation: a freighter bearing a cargo of agricultural fertilizer, of which the less said the better.

"You look wonderful, both of you," my dear Mary told us when at last we arrived in Strafford. "Especially you, Brinnie. You have a marvelous suntan, you're quite fit and trim. I knew a sea voyage would do you a world of good. But I'd begun to worry a little. I expected you home before now."

I replied that things were somewhat more complicated than I had supposed.

"They usually are," said Mary.

She wished to hear a full account. We refrained, nevertheless, from giving the details then and there of all that had happened, not wishing to cloud her loving welcome with retrospective anxiety. I merely remarked that our business had been successfully concluded.

"I'm glad to hear it," Mary said to me after Vesper went off to unpack. "It eases my mind considerably. I know you of old, my dear Brinnie. I sometimes fear you may lead the child into one scrape or other."

With all honesty, I assured Mary that such was not the case.

Since our return, I have given much private contemplation to the events in El Dorado. I have observed Vesper closely as she goes happily about her experiments in chemistry, plunking her banjo, or frolicking with Moggie, and my thoughts continually return to Ocotalpa.

I willingly accept an active volcano, mistakenly considered extinct, erupting unpredictably. Why it did so at that given moment troubles me. Mere coincidence, the idea that it would have happened with or without Vesper's presence is logical—but unsatisfying. It is, of course, totally unreasonable even to consider that Vesper had any influence whatever. And yet—

"You have the oddest look on your face, Brinnie," Vesper observed while I was in the midst of pondering that question. "What's bothering you?"

It was, I replied, an idle thought, a passing fancy not worth discussing.

There are limits to human capabilities and willpower.

Still, I am not certain how far those limits apply to Vesper. If at all.

It is reassuring, however, to know that volcanoes do not exist in her immediate vicinity.

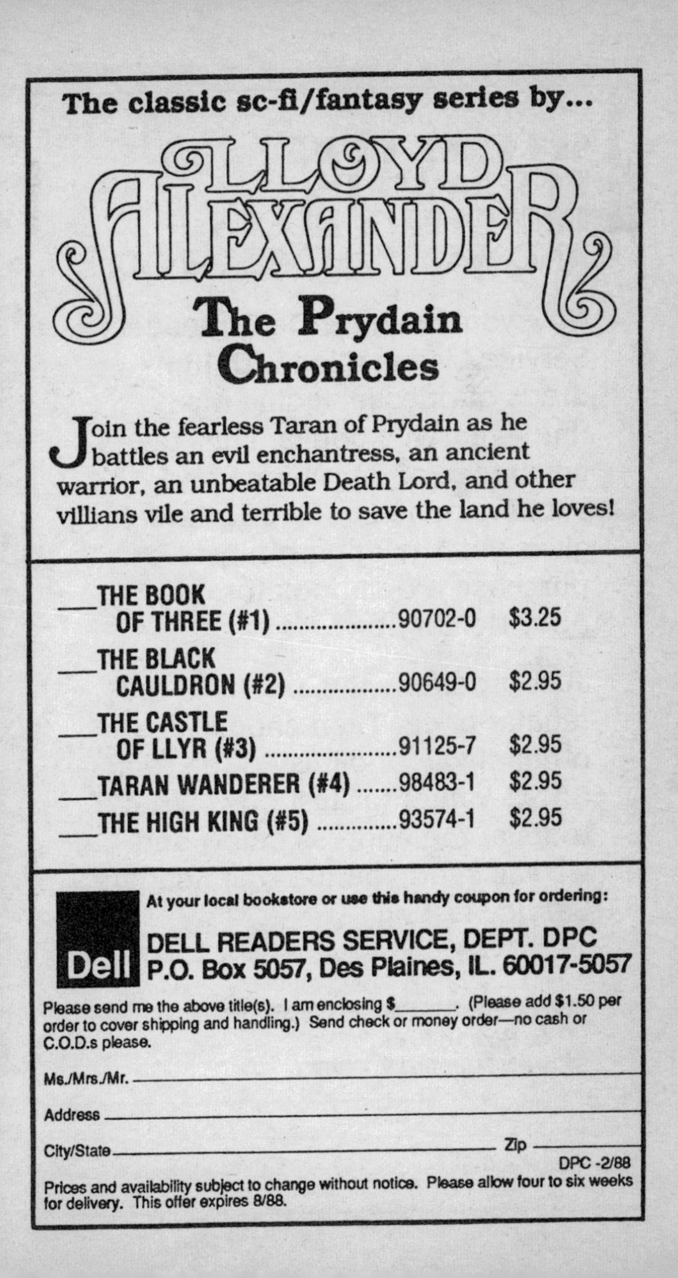
The classic sc-fi/fantasy series by...
LLOYD ALEXANDER
The Prydain Chronicles
Join the fearless Taran of Prydain as he battles an evil enchantress, an ancient warrior, an unbeatable Death Lord, and other villians vile and terrible to save the land he loves!
___THE BOOK OF THREE (#1) 90702-0 $3.25
___THE BLACK CAULDRON (#2) 90649-0 $2.95
___THE CASTLE OF LLYR (#3) 91125-7 $2.95
___TARAN WANDERER (#4) 98483-1 $2.95
___THE HIGH KING (#5) 93574-1 $2.95
Dell
At your local bookstore or use this handy coupon for ordering:
DELL READERS SERVICE, DEPT. DPC
P.O. Box 5057, Des Plaines, IL. 60017-5057
Please send me the above title(s). I am enclosing $______. (Please add $1.50 per order to cover shipping and handling.) Send check or money order—no cash or C.O.D.s please.
Ms./Mrs./Mr.
Address
City/State
Zip
DPC -2/88
Prices and availability subject to change without notice. Please allow four to six weeks for delivery. This offer expires 8/88.